I FOUND
HAPPINESS & TRAGEDY

Inspired by Milne, Hughes, Christie, & Poe

Selections from the 2022
Literary Taxidermy Writing Competition

Edited by

MARK MALAMUD

.

I Found Happiness & Tragedy

All stories & poems © 2022 by their respective authors
Anthology © 2022 by Regulus Press
"Five Years of Literary Taxidermy" © 2022 by Mark Malamud
Cover art © 2022 by Andrea Bollum

First Regulus Press printing November 2022
Signal Library 10-2202-01-21

Regulus Press, Seattle WA
www.regulus.press

ISBN: 173609744X
ISBN-13: 978-1-7360974-4-1
(Regulus Press)

This anthology is dedicated to all those brave and enthusiastic writers and poets who have participated in the Literary Taxidermy Writing Competition over the past five years. Challenges are meant to be faced, hills are meant to be climbed, and words are meant to be written.

CONTENTS

Introduction

Five Years of Literary Taxidermy

Welcome to *I Found Happiness & Tragedy*, the eighth anthology of literary taxidermy. This volume marks the fifth anniversary of the Literary Taxidermy Writing Competition and collects the twenty prize-winning stories and poems from 2022.

So what *is* literary taxidermy?

Literary taxidermy is a creative process that starts by taking the first and last lines from a classic work of fiction—a novel, short story, or poem—and then "re-stuffing" what goes in-between those lines to create a new and wholly-original work. The goal of the literary taxidermist is not just to slap someone else's words onto the start and finish of an otherwise stand-alone or preconceived story or poem, but to let the borrowed lines, absent any preconceived notions, summon—like a magical spell—the narrative that will fall between them. The result is a story or poem whose first and last lines are seamless, integral, and in fact the perfect start and finish to the new work.

Although this year marks the fifth anniversary of the Literary Taxidermy Writing Competition, the *idea* of literary taxidermy came into being nearly twenty years ago. I was looking for a writing exercise to fill time between projects. I knew only that I needed some sort of prompt, or constraint, to keep the exercise simple and self-contained; and that I wanted to try something I hadn't done before. I started staring into space (woolgathering), then spinning in my office chair (daydreaming), and then eventually I started pulling books from my bookshelf, looking for inspiration.

I opened Ian Fleming's *Casino Royale*—hadn't read it for years!—and re-read the novel's opening sentence. I was immediately struck by how well it worked as the start for the James Bond series. Out of curiosity, I flipped to the book's end. When I read the last line, my heart skipped a beat. The last line was *nothing* like the first—it was shocking, really—and it took me a few moments to remember the arc of the plot that led to that unexpected but perfect conclusion. I remember spinning in my chair, thinking how unlikely it was that that first line could lead to the last. But Fleming had done it. I'm a puzzle person. I love solving puzzles. So I wondered—idly, really—how might *I* do that? How would I get from that start to that finish?

And then it hit me: *Well, why not give it a try!*

I grabbed a pen (yes, I used pen and paper back then) and I started writing. Within an hour I had a draft of "Beatrice Dalle," the first literary taxidermy story. A few days later, I grabbed another book off my bookshelf—this time it was *In Watermelon Sugar* by Richard Brautigan—and started my second. Over the next year, I found myself going back to the idea again and again. I started pulling in other writers to give it a try, including Paul Van Zwalenburg, who would become the future editor of the 2019 literary taxidermy anthology *Pleasure to Burn*. I was clearly hooked.

A few years after I began experimenting with literary taxidermy, I collected my favorites in an anthology called *The Gymnasium*. Eighteen stories, each inspired by a different writer. I borrowed first and last lines from Stephen Crane, HP Lovecraft, Tom Robbins, Margaret Atwood, and others. But even before it was published, I began staring into space (daydreaming) and spinning in my chair (woolgathering) and eventually I wondered about *another* kind of collection. What would happen if rather than having a single writer tackle the first and last lines of a variety of classic works, you had a *variety* of writers tackle the *same* lines?

Thus was born the Literary Taxidermy Writing Competition, sponsored by Regulus Press. The competition invites writers to stitch together their own stories and poems using the opening and closing lines of specific works of fiction. For past competitions, participants were challenged by a variety of texts: *The Thin Man* written by Dashiell Hammett; *Through the Looking-Glass* by Lewis Carrol; "A Telephone Call" by Dorothy Parker; *Fahrenheit 451* by Ray Bradbury; *Beloved* by Toni Morrison; *Brave New World* by Aldous Huxley; and two works by New Zealand modernist Katherine Mansfield.

This year, the competition gave participants four choices for their literary taxidermy, taking lines from "As I Grew Older," a poem by Langston Hughes; "Ms. Found in a Bottle," a short story by Edgar Allan Poe; "Happiness," a poem by A. A. Milne; and "The Tragedy at Marsdon Manor," a short story by Agatha Christie. Writers had to create a short story or poem that starts and ends with the same sequence of opening and closing words as one of those four classic works.

This means, of course, that every piece in the present anthology starts and ends in one of four ways; but *the path* that each author takes from beginning to end is unique— and therein lies a particular thrill of reading these short works: despite sharing a common frame, they are all *different.*

So some of the stories and poems in this collection are funny, some are serious, some are heart-warming, some are scary, and some are just *strange.* They are filled with both happiness and tragedy. They cross genres; they cross continents; and they vary in style and diction and tone and voice. Reading each one is like getting a peek at the results of someone else's Rorschach test.

The authors are eclectic, too. They range in age from 25 to 78. Four have never been published before. They also span the globe, so you're about to read stories from the US, Australia, New Zealand, Japan, Canada, India, Ireland, Wales, and Scotland. (And that's why you may notice stories written in British or American English—so don't be shocked to find *colour* in one story and *color* in the next.)

The winning author in this year's poetry contest is Trudi Petersen, a nurse and shop-owner living in Wales in the UK. Her submission, "Valparaiso," is a poignant story of love, both lost and found. It captures in a mere thirty-nine lines something that is romantic, wistful, heartbreaking, and ineluctably human. Poe's first and last lines frame the narrative perfectly, and the piece is an excellent example of the transformative power of literary taxidermy.

The winning author in this year's short story contest is Clare Kate Mahon, an Irish teacher and doctoral student living in Cambridge in the UK. Her submission, "The Stone," tells a story that, like Petersen's poem, is centered on a kind of human anguish, but it does so through the lens of fantastic fiction. Death pays a visit to the elderly protagonist, but his arrival isn't so much macabre as melancholic, even comforting. Langston Hughes' first line provides an easy way into the story; and his last, an ambiguous ending perfectly suited to the tale. The piece demonstrates how one can be surprised by a story, despite knowing beforehand exactly how it starts and ends.

All the stories and poems in this anthology were selected by the editors at Regulus Press. The winning entries were selected by a panel of eight professional-writer judges. After each piece, you'll find a short biographical note about the author, and maybe—just maybe—*you* can figure out how they ended up writing the story or poem they did!

Mark Malamud
12 November 2022

(Oh, and the name of the anthology? It's a little bit of a puzzle, too, I suppose. It's a mash-up of the four titles from which this year's first and last lines were taken.)

Part I—A. A. MILNE

All the stories and poems in this section were inspired by the first and last lines from "Happiness," a poem by A. A. Milne, first published in *When We Were Very Young* in 1924.

John had great big waterproof boots on.

→

And that (said John) is that.

Jessica Grene

Highly Flammable

John had great big waterproof boots on. Pure white, like all the regulation boots on the floor. No one was allowed on the floor without putting them on. No one was allowed to clock out without taking them off, and leaving them for the sluice. John's were the biggest size, not many of those. When the girls started, there weren't any boots in their size. Had to be ordered special. Just two pairs, they stood out, smaller and whiter than the others. Never had any women on the floor before. It wasn't really heavy work, since automation, but men had always done it. The only women around the place had worked in the offices and the canteen. The system showed if anyone on the shift hadn't clocked out yet, but John still tallied the boots waiting for the sluice before he left at the end of the shift. Always had.

When John started out, it was only Irish in the whole place. Now there was nearly nobody on the floor that wasn't Brazilian. They'd do the job for less, didn't complain, worked hard.

Irish complained about not finding a job. They're not looking hard enough (said John).

There was a blind spot from the cameras. A few years back, a couple of lads had gone in there for a smoke. They'd been let go, not for bunking off but for smoking on the floor. Fires could devastate the place in a flash. They'd be cut off in that corner, and someone would risk their lives going in after them.

John had seen a fire, early on. Some of the lads thought it was harsh for them two to lose their jobs over going for a

15

smoke, but John wasn't in agreement. He said nothing. He told every new starter how the lads had lost their jobs for having a smoke, miming taking a drag, and showing 'out' with a pointing finger. He didn't tell them about the blind spot. Nobody but Farrell that was here now would know about that, unless the lads from security let on about it. John told the workers they were on camera all the time.

The lads he went to school with had moved on. They'd gone off to Dublin or Cork or Galway. They only came back at Christmas or for funerals. They'd come into Mulligans for a pint and be delighted to see John at the bar, instantly recognisable by the big bulk of him. Good man, Johnno, they said, as though they'd been friends throughout the school years. As though they'd ever called him anything but Thicko or gobshite.

They'd ask John what was the craic, Brady's, sure you're running the place by now, the mammy says there's only foreign lads in the place these days, Brazilians is it?

The classmates are baffled if Anders or Rafa greets John by name at the bar. Jaysus, never thought there'd be black lads working in Brady's.

These men are gratified that John's still at Brady's, as he was when they left the town. They're pleased that that Mulligan's pub hasn't changed. They want the town to stay the same, with the factory as its beating heart. They left. Their children go to college, travel abroad, have never set foot on a factory floor. But they want Irish people from the town to work in Brady's.

Women didn't go for jobs on the floor much. Easier waiting tables, cleaning, childcare. The two girls on his shift were well able for the work. Dolores was a strong, bony woman with cropped grey hair, who laughed and talked shit with the lads. Helena was quieter. She was heavy, her rounded flesh drooping on her body. Her face sagged downwards as well. John wasn't sure if from unhappiness, or just that was the set of it. He'd not had much contact with her. He saw himself in her. Not getting the joke, not moving quickly. He felt revulsion and compassion.

Even starting out, when there was plenty of other lads that spoke English, John wasn't a big talker. He didn't have an easy way with him. He felt lonely some days now, with no chats at all. He'd say things to himself, inside his head. No point saying them out loud. Some of the lads had decent English, but they weren't used to his way of talking. If you repeat "Grand day" three times before it's understood, you realise it was a useless thing to say in the first place.

He let the words in the locker room wash over him, listening to the tone of them, the laughter. The boys greeted him in English, but went back to chatting. Only other English speaker around was Dualta Farrell. Like John, Farrell was a safety officer because he was Irish. John hadn't much to say to Farrell. John came in early so he wouldn't arrive the same time as Farrell. Farrell would talk as they got out of their cars next to each other. His talk did John's head in. He'd talk about girls, say things about foreigners. He'd talk till they got in the door, and the lads'd see them arrive together.

I don't exactly know how I know this (said John), but there's something off about Farrell. Even to himself, he couldn't put into words the wrongness he saw. There was a cruelty to him; a hidden violence that John could see looking out of Farrell's eyes. He talked his shite to John, because he knew John didn't like it. He knew John would never tell him to shut the fuck up.

John didn't think the lads gave the girls a hard time. He couldn't understand the words, but listened to the sounds of their chatter. There was back and forth, but never had the ring of badness to it. They weren't young women. They weren't pretty. They'd not been able to find other work. Dolores was too butch, Helena too pathetic. The girls and some of the lads had to drive up from the town to Dublin nightly for their English classes, otherwise their visas wouldn't be renewed. The language school wouldn't give them their money back, let them study somewhere local.

He saw Farrell saying something to the girls. Dolores nodded, said something back. Helena nodded too, didn't look at Farrell, her eyes staring as if resisting turning to see his face. Farrell moved on, but later John saw him watching Helena, studying her like she was a menu, and he was going to order.

Not my business (said John). I know nothing.

Helena got quieter. John saw her movements, slow and dragging, when she put on the white boots to go on the floor. Her shoulders were more slumped. Farrell was oilier somehow, puffed up in himself. But there was nothing for John to know. Same as him, Farrell was on the floor the whole time.

Besides checking everyone was clocked out, John always checked the rack of boots for the sluice. Counted them. Knew straight off that the girls were gone, because the smaller white boots were there.

Better than computers, it showed him the floor was clear.

He left off the boots, put his shoes on. Helena came off the floor. She had black runners on her feet.

"Hey, Helena. You're clocked out. You can't go back on the floor without the boots on."

Her face was miserable. He thought he'd never seen a face look so ugly, and it made it worse than if she had been beautiful. Going back on the floor without PPE, not clocked in, was a serious incident, and he was supposed to write anyone up who did it. Not just the contamination, but the risk. Again and again in the safety videos. Fires from the dryers could spread in seconds, anyone on the floor could pass out from the smoke and die, nobody knowing they were there.

"Sorry," she said, keeping walking.

"Are you okay?" was all he said. He didn't know how to ask, what to ask. He didn't have the courage to help her. He read contempt in her eyes.

"Yes," she said crisply. "I go now."

The boots were all there. But he felt sure Farrell was lurking on the floor, planning to sneak out once John left. John wasn't going to say a thing about Helena. But he would write Farrell up.

Safety first (John would say) I can't let this go. You could have died.

Farrell would know John had seen Helena. John would say nothing. Farrell would leave Helena alone.

John waited.

After twenty minutes, the fire alarm sounded. The lights and clanging were impossible to ignore. John had done the drills so many times the actions were in his body, like putting on his boots. Farrell did not emerge from the floor.

The workers filed out, grinning, not sure whether to believe the supervisors telling them that this was not a drill. Excitement rose as heat and noise drifted from the back where the dryers were. They lined up and checked off names. John stood alone.

"Your shift's finished, yeah?" said the manager. "All of your team off the floor, out of the building?"

"That's right," said John. "All clocked out. Counted the boots."

"Thank fuck for that. This is a big one, no joke."

I didn't know he was there (said John) I had no way of knowing.

Flames were engulfing the back of the building. The manager shouted to go on home, lads, nothing to be done here, no use standing gawping.

John walked to his car. Farrell's car was parked in its place nearby.

And that (said John) is that.

"Highly Flammable"

JESSICA GRENE is a research program manager living in Dublin, Ireland. She has two young children, has drafted her first novel, and is working on another. She has been previously published in *Crannóg* literary journal and *Mslexia* magazine.

She says: "The boots of Milne's first line brought to mind white factory safety boots I've seen. I mixed in some experiences I've heard from Brazilian people working in Ireland and took it in a dark direction. As a country, Ireland has changed very rapidly in a short period of time and has a relatively recent history of immigration. And while it's not exclusive to Ireland, there is a strongly embedded capacity in this country for knowing or suspecting something without speaking out; I find this fascinating to write about."

Philip Amat

Ritual Pleasures

John had great big
Waterproof boots on
Emily had a bright red hat
Sarah wore next to nothing at all
And that (said John) is that

Emily brought
The silver handcuffs
Sarah, the familiar wombat
John forgot éclairs au chocolat
(How typical is that!)

Sarah lay down
On top of the sheets
John stood at the foot of the bed
Emily struggled to remember her lines
—Nothing at all was said

"How many times
Do I have to remind
You? How many times since we've wed?
Why the hell can't you get this stuff right!"
Whiskers (the wombat) said

John had great big
Waterproof boots on
Emily had a bright red hat
Sarah wore next to nothing at all
And that (said John) is that

"Ritual Pleasures"

PHILIP AMAT is a construction manager, living in the Pacific Northwest in the United States. Although he tells us that his day job keeps him busy, he is also an amateur antiquarian, an occasional equestrian, and a late-night writer. His work has been previously published in various journals, including *Night Shade*, *Piaffe*, *The Kingsland Review*, and *Saratoga Letters*.

He says: "My poetry is usually quite measured, but something about Milne's lines ignited a surprising playfulness in me. I was stumped for a while after the first stanza appeared, since it started and ended with Milne's first and last lines; but after a few moments the rest of the piece just tumbled out."

William Sharp

Colder Than Ice Cream

John had great big waterproof boots on, making it sound like he was stomping as he walked down the hall toward Caleb's room. Caleb recognized the sound because John wore them every weekend for his job at the mill. Usually, their mom would yell at John to take the damn boots off in the house before he ruined the wooden floors, but not this morning. *She must be sleeping in,* thought Caleb as he curled up a little tighter and pulled the covers over his head.

John rapped twice on Caleb's door before throwing it open.

"Get up, squirt! I need your help with something."

Caleb groaned and rolled under the covers toward the wall. "No. I'm still asleep. Do it yourself."

"No can do," said John, his boots booming across the floor to Caleb's twin bed. "It's a two-man job—well, one man, and whatever you are," he said, ripping the blanket and sheet back to expose the first-grader curled up in his t-shirt and shorts.

"Go away! You're buggin' me!" protested Caleb as John grabbed one bony ankle and dragged him off the bed onto the floor.

"Tough titties," replied John, releasing Caleb and returning to the bedroom door. "But if you help, there's an ice cream in it for you—my treat."

Caleb stopped rubbing his sore hip and sat up. "Ice cream? Really?"

"Really—*if* you pick your skinny ass up and get dressed."

John leaned on the door frame and drummed his fingers on it a couple of times. "I'll bring my truck around front. Get movin'."

Caleb jumped into a pair of jeans and sneakers, then ran to the kitchen and grabbed a fruit bar and juice box. John's pickup truck rumbled around the corner of the house, stopping at the porch. Caleb scrambled down the steps and hopped into the cab.

"Mighty nice of you to bring me breakfast," said John, making a grab for Caleb's fruit bar. Caleb had anticipated this, and hugged the bar to his chest while unwrapping it.

"No way. You coulda' got your own. Tough titties."

John smirked briefly at Caleb before gunning his truck onto the road.

It had been a while since John had taken Caleb for a ride in the truck. John had pretty much trashed it since their dad died, getting food stains on the seats, and leaving empty cans and butts all over the floor. The seats were still frayed and the dashboard still worn, but Caleb saw that all the trash was gone, and even some of the stains had been scrubbed clean. Caleb decided it was safe to poke the tiger, and chose a phrase he'd heard their mom use again and again.

"Looks like you finally got off your lazy ass and cleaned up the truck." He risked a glance at his brother. "Must've been for your date last night with *Re-bec-caaaa*," he teased in childish singsong from the relative safety of the other side of the truck's cab.

"Yeah. For my date," said John flatly. "With her."

John and Rebecca had started dating almost a year ago, the summer after his junior year. Caleb met her briefly then, after one of John's football games. John and Rebecca were holding hands while people took pictures of them: John in his football gear, Rebecca in her cheerleader uniform and wearing a little crown.

From the start, their mom didn't like Rebecca. She said she was "rich" and "snobby." This enraged John, and they had argued viciously about her, upsetting Caleb and causing him to hide in his room with his hands over his ears. Soon after, Rebecca stopped going out with John. Caleb hadn't seen her after that—until John's surprise date last night.

Caleb grinned mischievously. "I think mom must've already went to bed last night, but I was still awake. I was watching through my window. I saw you drive in with her—into the barn," he said, proud of his cleverness.

"I know," said John, staring at the road ahead. "I saw you, too."

"Did y'all 'make out' in the barn?" Caleb teased, not understanding exactly what that was, other than something people did on dates.

"Shut up," said John.

Not finished yet, Caleb sucked hard on the tiny juice box straw to annoy John with the irritating rattle of the last few drops. When he dropped the empty box on the floorboard John glanced down at it, and then quickly around the cab.

"Pick that up, shithead. And that wrapper, too." John motioned toward both. "Throw 'em out the window."

Caleb sighed dramatically and complied, the wind blowing his hair back from his forehead until he rolled the window back up. He watched the scenery go by for several minutes before turning again to John.

"Where're we goin'?"

"I—have to dump some trash."

Caleb nodded in approval. The dump was about five miles outside of town, and fun. They'd found some great stuff there, like the bike dad fixed up for Caleb, and a faded set of perfectly good aluminum lawn chairs. The place stunk like hell, but they sometimes got to shoot the possums that were everywhere, digging through the trash.

"You got your .22, John? We gonna' shoot some vermin?"

"Maybe. We'll see."

The truck sped down the highway for several minutes before turning onto an unmarked road that climbed higher into the hills and forest. John made a final turn onto a narrow gravel road, pulling off to the right and stopping.

"Alright, squirt, get out."

John stepped quickly to open the tailgate, pulling his ball cap down as he did. Caleb struggled to close the heavy passenger-side door before walking to the back of the truck where John stood at the tailgate putting batteries into what looked like two tiny radios. Caleb saw John's tool chest, some rakes and a shovel, and the spare tire in the truck bed, along with a big, dirty canvas sack. It looked to Caleb like one of the football team's equipment bags. It was pretty full, and kind of lumpy, like it was full of helmets.

Caleb turned to look at the unfamiliar surroundings.

"This ain't the dump, John."

John hadn't realized Caleb was there. He stuffed the walkie-talkies into his pockets and slammed the tailgate shut.

"I know it's not. I have to take care of something. It'll only take a few minutes. Next stop is the dump, I swear," John said, glancing around briefly. "C'mon. Stay close."

John and Caleb walked through the tall grass about fifty feet from the truck. He signaled Caleb to kneel, and they both hid behind some overgrown bushes.

"Alright, squirt, listen up." John showed Caleb the two walkie-talkies he'd been setting up back at the truck. "These are walkie-talkies. You use them to talk to someone far away." He gave one to the fascinated boy and showed him how they worked. Caleb was excited to hear his voice crackle from John's walkie-talkie. His thoughts raced as he imagined what fun he and his buddies would have with these when he got home.

John looked seriously at Caleb as he pointed back at the gravel road. "I need you to sit here and watch this road. If anyone follows me up this road, you take your walkie-talkie and hold down this button, and say right into here 'somebody's coming.' I'll answer with 'OK,' or something like that. But you *have* to stay hidden. Don't move from this spot for *anything*—you understand?"

Caleb nodded solemnly, hiding his excitement as John handed him a walkie-talkie. This was probably the coolest thing he had ever done, and about the easiest way to get ice cream he'd ever imagined.

John turned and stomped through the bushes in his big rubber boots, climbing quickly into his truck. He drove up the small road, into the woods, until Caleb could no longer see or hear the truck.

Caleb sat in silence, keeping his head low but peering through the bushes at the gravel road. Within just a few minutes this became incredibly boring, making Caleb think that maybe this *wasn't* the easiest way to get ice cream. He passed the time by examining every inch of the walkie-talkie, feeling the smooth black plastic case, admiring the silver telescoping antenna, and smelling the brand-new, genuine leather wrist strap. He dutifully checked for cars, but no one else drove by that morning. It felt like forever, but Caleb stayed hidden, and was relieved to see John's truck finally re-emerge from the woods. John didn't honk his horn, instead waving at Caleb to join him. Walkie-talkie clutched firmly in hand, Caleb climbed in and they drove away.

After they turned onto the highway, Caleb sat forward on the edge of the seat, arms crossed on the dashboard as he gleefully questioned John.

"Are we going to the dump now, John? And then for ice cream?"

"Yeah. Dump first. Then—ice cream."

Caleb returned to watching the trees and forest rush past the truck, grinning at it all. This was turning out to be the best chore John had every made him help with.

They turned off the highway and bounced along the pot-holed asphalt road that led to the dump. The familiar stench greeted them, making Caleb hold his nose and puff out his cheeks as he tried to avoid inhaling the disgusting smells of rot and decay. John drove through the open gate and then along the narrow path between huge piles of trash—thousands of plastic bags dotting mounds of twisted, rusty metal, soggy cardboard, and broken furniture.

"Look, John! A possum!" yelled Caleb, pointing outside John's window at the mottled, rat-like scavenger. He was disappointed that John didn't even look.

The truck skidded to a stop at the foot of another huge pile of garbage. John got out, waving off the cloud of flies that descended on him, and swiftly climbed the side of the trash heap, shoving and kicking pieces of the disgusting debris out of his way.

Caleb watched this curious behavior from inside the cab, then turned to check the truck bed for the canvas bag he assumed they'd be dumping here. He was surprised to see it was no longer there. He turned back toward John and saw him standing about ten feet up the side of the mound, motioning at Caleb to come join him.

Caleb jumped from the truck and ran to the trash pile, swatting at the flies, and climbing unsteadily to where John was waiting. He expected John to show him some varmint, or maybe some neat junk he had found. Instead, John was just standing there, holding open the door of a rusted old refrigerator that was lying on its back, half-buried in the trash. The shelves were missing, but the freezer compartment door was still closed.

Caleb looked at John, confused.

"What's this?"

"Your ice-cream," said John, staring vacantly at Caleb.

Caleb looked doubtfully down into the empty refrigerator, then back up at John.

"It's there, in the freezer," pointed John. "Just like I promised. See for yourself."

Caleb stepped hesitantly down into the refrigerator, bending over to open the freezer compartment door and see what was inside.

John let go of the door and watched it drop onto the boy, knocking him down and trapping him inside. The rusty chrome handle clicked as the heavy door latched, sealing the refrigerator closed forever.

John pulled some scrap plywood over the refrigerator, and threw some broken cinderblocks on top for good measure. He paused a few seconds to survey his work, seemingly oblivious to the muffled pounding.

Satisfied, John picked his way carefully down the mound of garbage, brushing off his hands, jeans and sneakers as he walked back to the truck.

"And that," said John, "is that."

"Colder Than Ice Cream"

WILLIAM SHARP is an administrative law judge living in Texas in the United States. When not writing science fiction and horror, he's busy working, playing with his grandkids or wife, and embarrassing his children (or so he tells us). He plays drums and guitar and sings in an amateur rock band, loves hiking, and loathes yardwork. He has previously self-published his fiction, and was an honorable mention in the 2021 Literary Taxidermy Writing Competition.

He says: "The basic story came to me within a few minutes of reading the Milne selection. I wrote it in a week while on vacation at the beach, as my best writing happens away from the distractions of home. The first draft took three weeks to edit down to 2000 words. I had to frequently stop, apologize to Milne, and remind myself that I am not a psychopath. When my wife finished reading the story and looked at me warily, and my son said it was his least favorite of my stories, I knew I was onto something."

Isobel Cunningham

Amor Vincit

John had great big waterproof boots on.
Jill wore her hat with flowers and fruits on.
They looked at each other and thought, How Odd!
No mirrors at home? I mean, my God!
To be seen like that, it's a crime against *Vogue*.
And I've heard it said he's a bit of a rogue.
But our Jill was struck by his eyes of black
And he couldn't take his eyes off her rack
on the back of her car where she'd hung her bike.
John loved a spin, so he asked if she'd like
a drink or a coffee or a tandem ride.
"All right then, John, we're on!" she cried.

All spring and summer and in the fall
they pedalled away till they heard the call
of Canada geese flying off down South.
"Winter's coming," said John and he noticed her mouth
was as red as a berry and her hair as bright
as the leaves on the trees and the stars of the night
found a home in her eyes. So he held her hand
and declared that he loved her to beat the band.
Of course, Jill said yes, they could soon be wed
if only he'd lose those boots. But John said
he couldn't let go of his waterproof boots
or wear some fancy tailor-made suits.

"I love you, Jill, with your birds-nest hair,
your eyes and your lips and this fine pair
of boots will always mean I can be me."
"All right" said Jill "as long as I'm free
to wear my hat with the cherries and flowers."
And the following week the words, "By the powers,"
were read out quick by the parson and clerk
who blessed them both and made short work
of the prettiest wedding you ever did see.
For as John put it, "My Jill and me…
are Romeo 'n' Juliet, the sun and the moon.
A sweet sweet melody sung in tune.
We're the east and the west, the sea and the land.
We're our meant-to-be, our ever-clasped hand.
We're more than a boot and more than a hat.

And that, said John, is that!

"Amor Vincit"

ISOBEL CUNNINGHAM is an English teacher and retired hospital social worker living in Montreal, Canada. Her grandkids used to call her the "story machine" and pretend to feed her quarters and crank her arm to get her writing. She loves being outdoors and tries to defend nature as much as she can. She has been previously published in *The Blue Nib Literary Magazine* and in the annual anthology for the Scottish Arts Trust Story Awards.

She says: "I love A. A. Milne and I like poems that have a framework of rhythm or rhyme scheme. I have written plenty of free and blank verse, but I was able to really have fun with this one. It took me only a day or so to write. I was staying with my daughter on Vancouver Island, so I was enjoying a light-hearted holiday atmosphere. I had to keep on saying the poem out loud to be sure it worked—almost like a song."

Annamaria Formichella

Cold Comfort

John had great big waterproof boots
on, and a lopsided smile, like he just
couldn't believe he had fallen out of
the boat. You know how sometimes

you laugh at a tragic moment—some
kind of short circuit happens in your
brain. The day we told our youngest
the old dog had been put to sleep, she

snorted out a loud barking chortle and
immediately stepped backward down
the dark hallway as if to hide from her
own teenage insensitivity. But we knew

such giggles were the combined shock
of love and loss coming out the only way
it knew how. Unlike the gray lake water,
which could find no way out of John's

heavy rubber boots—anchors now—
pulling him down to the zebra mussels
and long green reeds that waved from
the bottom like the silky hair of mermaids.

Perhaps it was their icy welcome that
inspired the shivery grin as he spat out
his last words before the water closed
without a ripple. And that (said John) is that.

"Cold Comfort"

ANNAMARIA FORMICHELLA is an English professor living in Iowa in the United States. Her interests include distance running, modernist literature, and mushroom pizza; but her true passion is writing. She loves the texture of words and the shiver of recognition that happens when you encounter language that moves you. She has had her fiction published in the *Knight Literary Journal* and *Wilderness House Literary Review*, and poems in *Toe Good Poetry* and *Gyroscope Review*.

She says: "I love the challenge of working against limitations when composing poetry. Restrictions function like the grain of sand in an oyster—you need the irritation to create the pearl. The opening line from the Milne poem pushed me in a dark direction that I didn't expect, which led me to the idea of conflicting reactions to an event. Having a somewhat rigid frame pushed me to write a poem I'm really proud of, one that's quite different from my other work."

Frank Ruscitti

Souvenirs

John had great big waterproof boots on. He wasn't sure why, but figured the alligator standing by the lift would likely fill him in.

"It's not what you'd think, I assure you," said the alligator. "Let's go."

They both stepped into the elevator, floor covered in blood and feces. Hence the boots, thought John.

"Um, no," said the alligator. "They're for the biting."

"The biting?"

"Everything bites where you're going," said the alligator. "Mostly around the ankles. Don't worry. The rest ain't bad. Broken glass aside, you'll get used to it." The alligator pressed the down button, and the doors closed quickly.

It took a while, but John did get used to it. He made peace with the heat and mastered the stench. Even the biting wasn't so bad—thank goodness for the boots! The free jazz was annoying, and okay, the meals were a little rough—there's no salt in Hell, I mean, *really*?—but all in all it was quite doable.

Until the tourists started showing up.

"Look! An alligator!" screamed a small group in matching baseball caps, snapping photos with their iPhones. Soon, souvenir shops opened; one could buy *My Parents Went to Hell and All I Got Was This Lousy T-Shirt* shirts and artisanal local food products, all 'extra spicy.' Italian restaurants hawked menu *touristicos* that featured *vetro piu rotto del inferno*. Living statues sprang up in every corner, including an excellent Adolph Hitler and Bernie Madoff, collecting coins from unsuspecting tourists who didn't realize that it really was Hitler and Madoff.

"How's your day going?" asked Hitler, on a break.

"Getting a little stiff," said Madoff.

Then things escalated. The reviews came in and they were fabulous. Travel blogs were over the moon, giving pluses for the ankle biting ("Great fun!") and the heat ("Bring your bathing suit!"), but minuses for the food ("Could be better"). What started as an off-the-beaten-track vacation soon became Trip Advisor's number one hot spot. The crowds responded. Hell was hotter than ever.

This success, however, did not go over well with some.

"What the flying fuck!" shouted an angry denizen. This may have been Hell, but it was their Hell. They worked hard to be here, and suddenly anyone with a Fodor's book could come and visit. "It's just not right!"

The devil sat looking at his minions thoughtfully. On the one hand, he got it. Fire and brimstone! Used to be if you had a ticket, you deserved it. Make it here, make it anywhere, he thought. Still, even if he couldn't admit it, old Beelzebub was loving it. We were now café society! His picture was on coffee mugs! Italian restaurants!

John stood up to speak.

"Look, Devil," he said, apprehensive but firm. "This is unhallowed. People are supposed to abhor this place. They're not supposed to want to go to Hell, remember? Now we've got couples putting padlocks on bridges!"

The Devil picked his nose. Looking at his snot, he knew John was right. One more tourist and Hell might freeze over. He scratched his ass.

"Suggestions?"

"Yeah," came a gruff voice from the back. The alligator ambled up to the front and the crowd got silent. "I got a suggestion."

The Devil smelled his finger.

The alligator said: "You want to get rid of these amateurs? Forever?"

Everyone in the crowd nodded.

"Make Hell hellier."

Hellier? thought John. That's not even a word.

"They want hot? We make it hotter," said the alligator. "Put in more staircases. Charge an actual arm and a leg. No more monthly passes. Double the price for a bottle of water. No more knee-high boots."

"No!" gasped the crowd. Everybody loved their boots.

"We," he said, tail swishing for dramatic effect, "have to make Hell the worst place on Earth, so to speak."

The crowd murmured nervously. The Devil sat back in his throne. I have been wanting to make some changes, he thought. This place hasn't been renovated since the *Mad Men* craze and was in dire need of updating. Maybe go more open concept?

"All right!" shouted the Devil. "Let's do this!"

So, the indwellers of the underworld went about making it worse. Upon entering, new visitors were smacked in the face with water balloons filled with vomit. It now cost a body part to ride the rides—two at the hotter attractions like Push Your Kid Down a Well. The price for The Ferry to Styx Experience was a child, who was given a free costume of their favorite Marvel character and then led to the alligator pen for feeding. Worst of all, the cost of bottled water *tripled*.

This did nothing to stop the tourists, however. Hell was more happening than ever.

"Hey, Bill, how many rides have you been on?" asked one tourist of another.

"Seven!" said the second, holding up three fingers. "How's the family? Timmy having fun?"

"Not sure," said the first tourist. "He, um, fell down a

well!"

They both laughed.

Families of four suddenly becauses families of three. Sales of refrigerator magnets and Planet Hollywood shot glasses doubled. At one point the organizers had to close the Sharp Stick in The Eye exhibition, because Hell had run out of sticks—it was *that* popular. Satisfaction indicators were through the roof, with customers giving high marks for everything except the food. Glamping became a thing.

Eventually, however, the good times had to run their course. The crowds began to thin. Even with its warm climate and now world-renowned attractions, tourists, always looking for an industry gamechanger, started to get bored. They stopped coming. Buses were now half-filled; unsold water bottles melted everywhere.

"Where is everybody?" asked John. The alligator shrugged. The Devil slumped in his chair.

"Short shelf-life," said the alligator. "People want the next big thing and that was us for a while, but not anymore."

"But—*where did they go*?" asked John. He was dejected. He had way too many leftover sticks and few eyes left to poke.

The Devil brooded. He had to put on a good front; this was best for Hell, blah, blah, blah, kneel before me, etc. etc. He couldn't show, however, that he really was disappointed. He'd hit his stride in the last couple of months. Now all he had were memories.

"Where? The *other place*," he said, hocking up a mouthful of phlegm. "Excuse my French, but God knows why! Clouds and harps, and—holy moly—everybody with that blond hair. It's The Carpenters twenty-four seven!"

Secretly a big fan, the alligator nodded his head in agreement. Suddenly it came to him. He was tired. They all were. It had been nothing but work, work, work for the last couple of months. His head hurt, and his soul needed a break.

"Hey, John. When was the last time you really took a vacation?"

The boy's eyes lit up. A vacation! How fun!

"I was still alive, to be honest," he replied.

The Devil jumped up in glee. The possibilities! he thought. He smacked his lips with delight and rose from his throne.

"I'm in!" said the Devil.

The alligator wagged his tail and started singing. "*I'm on the—top of the world—lookin'—down on creation….*"

"Remember. No eating people," said John. The alligator looked at the Devil. The Devil shrugged. "No sticks. No ankle biting. Agreed?"

"Agreed," said the Devil. He ran to pack his bags.

"Sure," said the alligator, not meaning it.

"I mean it," said John. The alligator snorted.

And that (said John) is that.

"Souvenirs"

FRANK RUSCITTI is a musician, actor, and writer living in Pennsylvania in the United States. He's been a rock 'n' roller since his sister took him to see the Beatles' *HELP!* at the tender (and impressionable) age of six, wrote his first songs at the age of ten, and made his debut at CBGBs in New York at the age of fifteen. "Souvenirs" is his first published story.

He says: "This story was partially inspired by a rock opera I wrote when I was sixteen: the tale of a young boy who goes to hell and wreaks havoc by starting a travel agency. I turned it in as a high school project with libretto, lyrics, and a cassette filled with acoustic guitar versions of the songs. I got an A. The idea has obviously stuck with me and now, forty-five years later, it's re-emerged as this piece. It would make for a great TV pilot. (Netflix, are you listening?!?)"

Part II—LANGSTON HUGHES

All the stories and poems in this section were inspired by the first and last lines from "As I Grew Older," a poem by Langston Hughes, first published in *The Weary Blues* in 1926.

It was a long time ago.

→

Help me to shatter this darkness, to smash this night, to break this shadow into a thousand lights of sun, into a thousand whirling dreams of sun!

The Stone

It was a long time ago, so Nathan is not particularly surprised to see Death sitting at his kitchen table.

Nor is he especially alarmed.

Death sips his coffee—black, neatly made in one of Nathan's small, white cups—and smiles pleasantly at him. His teeth are straight and white, glinting sharply in the setting sun. His suit borders on cartoonish, crisp and clean in a way that looks uncomfortable.

Death seems more familiar than he had expected.

Sighing, Nathan slides his shoes off at the door, his slippers comforting and homely. He sets his worn-out trainers next to the unfamiliar dress shoes. "Are you here for me?" He doesn't sound upset.

He supposes he isn't.

Death raises his eyebrows, takes another sip of his drink. The silence is disrupted by the slight clink of the china against his teeth and the faded noise of traffic through the window. He casts his eyes around Nathan's small apartment over the rim of the cup as if to say, *who else?*

Nathan sighs again, too bone tired to play Death's little games. "I see."

He sets his bag on the floor and makes his way to the small kitchen, the coffee pot still warm. He pours himself a matching cup of coffee. The smell fills his senses, his thrumming mind going quiet.

He sits in the chair opposite Death, his slippers scuffing on the bare wooden floor. Silence fills the apartment again.

Not quite awkward, more unsure.

Death holds his gaze steadily, a small smile sketched onto the corner of his lips. Nathan's gaze slips from Death's lips up to his eyes, where something dances. Amusement, perhaps. Contempt, quite possibly.

Nathan refuses to break first.

Consider this his last great battle, declining to bow to Death's whim at his own dinner table. So, he takes a sip of his coffee, lets the flavour bathe his mouth in its cooly reassuring bitterness.

His hand trembles only slightly as it sets the cup back against the table, the sound skittering. Death lets out a slow breath. Nathan swallows.

"Do I know you?"

That causes Death to pause. He tilts his head, reminding Nathan. Tension quivers at the corner of his mouth, a question blossoming in the interested line of his shoulders.

"You look like a boy I used to know."

Death frowns. "I am not he." His voice is deeper than Nathan imagined, his tone clipped. "I'm not who you think I am."

He must get this a lot, Nathan thinks. He smiles. "I never said you were him. Just that you look like him." He takes another sip of his coffee, now past the point of lukewarm. "It doesn't matter, though. He went a long time ago." His hand is steadier now that his cup is lighter.

A strange silence settles over the two of them. Nathan revels in his small victory.

"I'm still not what you think I am," Death says, a little sulkily. He is looking out of the window, something in the distance lightly interesting to him.

Nathan feels his pulse at the base of his neck. He follows Death's gaze to the horizon, sees the sun slipping behind the curve of the earth.

"You're Death."

Death nods.

"You're here to kill me."

Death shakes his head. "I've only come to fetch you."

The words send a shiver up Nathan's neck, the fine hairs all over his body creeping awake. "I'm not ready."

He thinks about the neat pile of paper, the carefully arranged pens in his pen pot, the shiny new stapler he bought only last week, all waiting for him on his desk. He thinks about the emails that will slowly pile up in his inbox. He thinks about the man he sits opposite.

He remembers he left a yoghurt in the fridge for tomorrow. It'll go bad soon.

He really isn't ready.

"Shall we go for a walk?" Death is already standing up, collecting the two mostly empty coffee cups and carrying them over to the sink. Nathan sees he has a hole in the heel of one of his socks. The flesh that peeks out from the black cotton seems oddly vulnerable.

He looks up, sees Death watching him, waiting for a reply.

"Yes, let's."

Nathan is surprised when Death brings a jacket to the park.

The heavy clouds threaten snow—as they have for a few days now—but the chill doesn't reach his bones the way he remembers. He pushes his hands deeper into his pockets, pressing against the tissues he's been meaning to throw away.

A small girl streaks past them, screeching with laughter. Her cheeks are blooming in the cold air, her short hair unruly where it spills from her hood.

She doesn't notice Death smiling down at her.

"I used to come here, too, as a child," Nathan says, only partly to bring Death's attention back to him.

Death nods, looking away from the girl. "I know." A

breeze flutters around them, stinging Nathan's eyes. Death's hair lies still. "I was with you then, too."

Nathan's gaze finds the girl again, scrambling to join an older boy—her brother, perhaps—on the low branches of a nearby oak. Her voice is bright and demanding and full of vigour.

The boy pulls her up onto his branch where she wobbles, laughing delightedly. Nathan bites his tongue to stop himself calling out to her to be careful.

Falling is so very easy to do.

"You used to climb that tree." Death is watching him watch the children, something unreadable dancing across his face. "I remember you fell out of it once."

Nathan remembers.

The way the bark had scratched harshly against the soft skin at the back of his knee. The way his fingers had closed around empty air, clawing at nothing. The way his heart had constricted in his chest as he watched the leaves above him slowly shrink.

His mother's shout echoing in his ears, guilt swelling in his gut once again at his childish carelessness.

Strong arms of a boy not that much older than he was, firm enough just to break his fall and save his life.

He'd had some nasty cuts and a harsh telling off afterwards, but neither had bothered him much. He'd been too busy daydreaming about dark eyes and careful hands, too young to know why he felt the way he did, but old enough to know that it meant something.

"Somebody caught me," Nathan whispers. The girl is higher in the tree now, her brother's hand hovering protectively at her elbow.

He wishes somebody would catch him now.

The apartment is as they left it. The air feels stuffy after the cold freshness of the outdoors.

"I have a spare toothbrush," Nathan says once they are in the door. His back is pressed against the wall as Death hangs his jacket on a peg. In just his socks, he's a little shorter than Nathan.

Nathan presses his cheek to the wall, looking away. Call it self-preservation, perhaps.

Death moves away, his footsteps soft in the dark room. He watches wordlessly as Nathan readies himself for bed, as he moves through the routine he's engraved into himself.

Nathan brings a pillow and sheet and clean t-shirt to the sofa. He hovers awkwardly for a moment, a still-packaged toothbrush in his hand. He feels on show in his old, baggy pyjamas. "The bathroom is just over there." He points to the open door. "Let me know if you need anything else."

Death nods, accepting the toothbrush with a smile. "Thank you, Nathan. Sleep well."

Nathan tells himself it's not a threat.

The next morning, Nathan is smiling even before he can properly open his eyes.

Death calls from the kitchen. "Would you like some eggs?"

The kitchen smells warm in a way Nathan recognises. "My favourite," he remarks. "Did you sleep well?" It feels like an odd question.

Death just hums, tipping the contents of his pan onto two plates. "Did you?" The portion he sets in front of Nathan is significantly larger.

The eggs taste familiar. Nathan swallows, nodding. "Like the dead."

Death makes no comment.

"I'd like to go somewhere."

Death looks at Nathan over the edge of the book he is reading. It is a collection of poems a boy gave him for a birthday years ago. The spine has never been broken. He seems accepting of Nathan's whims. "Somewhere," Death muses. "Where would you like to go?"

Nathan is laid on the floor, looking up at a broken light he's been meaning to report for weeks. The wooden floor presses against his spine. The world seems impossibly large and scary in that moment.

"The ocean is beautiful this time of year."

Death closes his book. "Then we shall visit the ocean."

Nathan closes his eyes, the sound of his own breathing loud in his ears.

They are the only ones braving the beach today, the wind whipping around them possessively. Even the gulls are tucked up in their gull-beds, safe and warm and sensible.

"I want to swim," Nathan says to the horizon.

Death listens.

They pile their clothes safely on the shore; Death's neat suit next to Nathan's scruffy sweatshirt. They run into the unruly waves with a kind of determination, the icy water clinging to them coldly.

The chill draws a startled shout out of Nathan which the wind snatches for itself. The rocks under his feet are mostly smooth, worn by time and salt.

He lets himself float for a while, unwary of the tide. Death bobs beside him, face dark.

"Doesn't this make you feel alive?" Nathan asks.

"It makes me feel cold," Death whispers. He is holding a stone in his hands, small and round and perfectly formed. He turns it over and over in front of them, and Nathan can feel Death's eyelashes flickering as he watches the movement.

Nathan imagines the stone skittering away over the waves in front of them. He imagines the ripples spreading out across the water, before growing still or becoming waves on some other distant shore. He imagines the final *plop* as the stone sinks below the surface. Forever.

He shivers.

"Shall we go home?" Death's voice is light, his hand on Nathan's wrist gentle.

Nathan nods. "You should drive," he says tiredly.

They leave the sand at the beach, not a single grain sticking to them as they climb back aboard the moped. Everything is exactly as they left it, except the stone which Death pressed into Nathan's palm with a small smile.

Nathan leans his face against Death's back, unable to tear his gaze from the ocean. There is salt on his face. He's not sure where it came from.

His hands find one another as he clings tight. He doesn't put on his helmet.

He trusts Death to keep him safe.

Home.

The lights are welcoming, the feel of the key in the lock familiar.

"Are you cold?".

Nathan reaches out a hand to rest on Death's cheek. "You look so much like him," he says.

Death's features do not move. His breathing is very slow. "You miss him." He says the words slowly, as if the idea is unfamiliar to him.

Every day. Each and every day. Every time in a new way.

Even despite the warmth of the apartment Nathan shivers.

Death pulls him close. He smells like a room left empty for too long. Nathan is too tired to mind, closing his eyes gratefully.

Nathan murmurs his question, almost inaudible. "You'll

be there when I wake up? And then can you help me to shatter this darkness, to smash this night, to break this shadow into a thousand lights of sun?"

"Into a thousand whirling dreams of sun."

"The Stone"

CLARE KATE MAHON is an Irish teacher and doctoral student living in Cambridge in the United Kingdom. Her story, "The Stone," is told through the lens of fantastic fiction, but it remains very much centered in the human experience. Langston Hughes' first line provides an easy way into the story; and his last, an ambiguous ending perfectly suited to the tale. The piece is a thrilling example of literary taxidermy—and how one can be surprised by a story, despite knowing its precise start and finish. "The Stone" is her first published work. It was a joy to read and a pleasure to award.

She says: "My story is an homage to the children's picture book *Death, Duck and the Tulip* by Wolf Erlbruch. This book got me thinking: why is it that when we get older, Death is portrayed as a malevolent figure? I wanted to write a story for adults featuring Death as an intimate, capturing a sense of melancholy, but without fear."

Susan B Borgersen

So You Call This Progress, Said Mother

It was a long time ago—long before
linoleum kitchen floors
before pale pink and green Tupperware boxes
with damp sandwiches
for lunches

Before moving pictures moved into
living rooms
before Mary Pickford and
Fatty Arbuckle came to town

Mother's stories.

When women scrubbed their front stone steps
on rough-red knees
in the frost-dawn of each day
Steam rising from carbolic foam
and off their laboured backs

When men took their snap to the pit
in tin lunch pails
going down in the cage
going down the shaft
going down down down
with each clank of the gear
to the blackdamp coalface

The slippery slope she'd said

When the pit closed
when a fire could burn at a flick of a switch
when the clever wireless changed to radio
then on to this new age with no wires

And gas lamps were no longer lit by lamplighters

And the outside toilet was brought inside

Mother warns.

Progress flashing through decades
Without brakes
Without thought
Without protecting
What had gone before

It will come back she'd said
That idiot should never have taken up the railway lines
overburdening the roads with overloaded
overweighted lorries filled with nonsenses
for a throwaway society:
those who know not the difference between
need
and
want

They will learn that new is not always best
Remember the dark ages
that is what will return
when we have drained
our world of all it can possibly give

Mother's wisdom.

Prepare for the dark to come

She'd lived through a century of change
Her knowledge of what went before and how
wrong some things are now

She beckons me forward
to her sickbed pillow her lips trickle-moving
she whispers
Look for the sun, my darling, always seek the light—
the sun
yes—
the sun

Please do your bit, tell your world to look back behind the shadows
do this for me after I am gone
you must help me to shatter this darkness, to smash this night
to break this shadow into a thousand lights
of sun
into a thousand whirling dreams
of sun

"So You Call This Progress, Said Mother"

SUSAN B BORGERSEN is a retired IT professional, author, and poet living in Nova Scotia, Canada. When she was 11, she was taught by an air force sergeant to waggle her ears. She's also a knitter with 74 years of experience. In fact, she tells us she can knit and waggle her ears at the same time. She has previously published novellas, micro fiction, and poetry; and was an honorable mention in the 2020 Literary Taxidermy Writing Competition.

She says: "My mother died in March this year. She was 98. She'd seen it all. Embraced progress. Two months after her death I wrote this poem. Her voice was in my head. It was the opening line that brought to the fore many of the conversations we'd had over the decades. Hence the poem. I wrote it, holding my breath, capturing her wisdom, her hindsight, her voice, in one swift sitting, knowing the ending just had to be."

Erika Bauer

Because Cowboys Ride Horses into Sunsets

"It was a long time ago," came the voice from KCRX-AM Roswell, as it filled the Chevelle before spilling out into the New Mexican desert, "but it's still a classic. And we're bringin' it to you on our last broadcast. We thank you so much, folks. Here's Willie Nelson and Waylon Jennings telling all you Mommas out there, *Don't Let Your Babies Grow Up to Be Cowboys.*

James saw the valley of Eight Mile Draw far ahead in the distance, as they headed down Route 70 towards Las Cruces in need of divorce on account of Layla befriending Jim Beam like they were blood brothers and then falling in love with the sepia tones of a country bar after midnight, when the world is mellow and dusty calm. The whiskey made the man at the bar seem like a bearded James Dean resurrected from the dead, there to take Layla off into a world of white t-shirts billowing in the New Mexican sunlight. Thirteen hours later, though, at the Chapel of Crystals on a road called Paradise, the whiskey had long since left, and Layla found herself with a stranger named Billie and no white horse.

Willie Nelson could've told her. And James *did* tell her: Smoky old pool rooms *aren't* clear mountain mornings. And they never will be.

James watched the sun rise in the rearview mirror. Beneath him, the Chevelle's 145 thousand horses begged to be set free, as the tires galloped towards divorce, another kind of freedom, and the promise of rest and maybe a little bourbon, and the sun setting over the Chihuahuan Desert.

"It was a long time ago," he said, pointing out toward the valley. "The last time we were here. That gas station at Border Hill. Thought the owner was going to build you a house out in the desert, he was so taken with you. Those smoky eyes and black jeans. He never seen something so dark and so pretty walk off the edge of the earth like that."

Layla liked the way James told it, the way he saw that day, like the last chapter in a book you never finish since you know how that story ends anyway. No need to be disappointed twice, Layla reckoned. Just let the mirage fade on the back of your eyes, a shadow of nostalgia so sweet.

"He had that dog," she smiled. "I almost stayed just for that dog."

Willie Nelson knew about that too: little warm puppies *do* make you forget almost anything.

Looking out over all that empty space, the sound of two guitars harmonizing out of Roswell, James had the distinct feeling he'd been here before. He could almost taste the leather of the reins, feel the hard smoothness of the saddle of the horse he never rode.

"All little boys want to be cowboys," he said aloud, as if finishing an earlier thought.

"Cowboys always leave in the end, though. Don't they? Even the good ones." Her eyes drank in the same wide open space of the early morning valley, so vast and dry and flat you almost forgot it wasn't a painting, that you weren't a piece of still fruit in a bowl on the rim of the world. "Cowboys ride off into the sunset when the job is done. And someone is there to watch, enit?"

James had forgotten that Layla had been a little girl who waited on porches. He had forgotten the chorus of all the best cowboy songs because the refrain was just too pretty.

But still, he could see some version of himself coming down a distant hill on the back of a wild Mustang bred in the rain shadow of the desert-white body, gray legs and mane. It was the horse he saw as a little boy, outside his Momma's house, running free, as he played with his lasso and toy guns.

And now it was a Chevy—not a Ford, not a horse. And he was riding into some sunrise—not a sunset—on a mission of divorce for the only person who could chase away his silences with silence of her own.

"It was a long time ago," she said, as the sun illuminated his profile, "since last you spoke about him. Gotten to be so I can't remember the last time you said his name."

James' eyes never left the road. His breathing, like a metronome, kept steady. Even the pupils of his eyes knew how to comport themselves. He didn't have the words to explain, not even to Layla, who forever barred the door and manned the gate.

He had someone beautiful. And then he was gone.

And so they looked out at the mountains instead, at the big rolling clouds that threatened to float the very earth straight to heaven, knowing that soon it would be Mescalero, and then Bent, a place so small it could only be called a place. Had Willie Nelson been there to guide them, he'd have seen Bent for what it truly was: a small gathering of bodies suspended in an ocean of mountain made out of nothing but Lonestar belt buckles.

Beautifully barren and hard.

Since he couldn't say his name, James thought of a summer night instead. A bar outside Alamogordo, the very last set of the evening, a time when emotions taste like whiskey and whiskey tastes like yesterday. Layla was singing about constant sorrow, and James was playing like the guitar didn't need him, and the music was moving the lips of even the most lost. It was an ugly place made pretty for a moment by the sound of a voice and the strum of a guitar. It was then that James saw a tall man at the back of the bar grab hold of a woman's wrist. A tiny wrist on a suntanned arm. He watched the woman cry out as the man half-pushed, half-plowed her body up out of the barstool and into the wall.

And then he watched Mick get up slowly. He watched the tall man's boots appear to levitate as if God himself were calling him home. He watched the man's body return to earth and hit the floor, parting the carcasses of peanuts like a Red Sea of Shells. He watched Mick nonchalantly deposit the man in the dirt out front of Los Tres Gatos. He watched Mick quietly find his seat, smile and nod his head just once at James—all before the fourth verse.

If James hadn't known before, he knew then. He knew that night. After Layla, Mick was all he needed.

James rolled down the window. The heat crept in like a ghost of the sun, a tingling at the back of the neck, a caress on the face. The sound of Layla's voice brought him back to the road, to the approach of Mescalero. The song out of Roswell was still knocking around her head. In a half-hum, the words coming in and out of focus, she sort of sang, almost whispering Mick's name between the lines—*if you don't understand him…an' he don't die young…he'll prob'ly just ride away….*

As the hum washed over him, James tipped his head slightly out the window, and glanced above, his breath nearly stilled by the sight. The skies of Mescalero were so clean, so immaculate, it was as if God chose to rinse every paint brush in the universe, save one—the skies over Mescalero were brand new.

And so it was there, under that sky, when he said it.

"We haven't talked much about where we're going and why, Layla. How it came to be."

"You know how it came to be," she said. "I was drunk. He was nice. I got caught up. You know how that is, don't you? Getting caught up?"

"I know how that is," he said, his voice soft and low. "But this wasn't like you. Running off, getting married. You never run anywhere."

"No," she said. "I don't. Not after that first time at least. With you." She remembered walking off her front porch at seventeen, James standing in the driveway. No more walking Momma from the couch to the bed, worrying about tripping on bottles of Old Crow Kentucky Straight in the process. No more maneuvering round pill bottles on the carpet, kicking them like Chiclets in the darkness. And she remembered Momma's last words most of all, digging in to her head, trying to rope her back onto that porch, back into that tiny life: "That boy don't love you, girl. You can't see that? He may protect you and keep you but he ain't ever gonna *love* you like you love him." Layla could still see Vy laughing, could still feel the sting of alcoholic truth mixed with sickness cut with love: "He can't. There's no turning that boy."

Right then it was so hot in the car, Layla wanted nothing more than to pull over right there, walk clear to the Apache Reservation, find the nearest, most pristine lake and sink straight to the bottom.

Just the quiet and the clean and the cold.

Instead, though, she said it the best she could: "I was alone that night. You had gone off a few days before, kind of disappeared on account of Mick being gone. And I was there in that bar, without you, and I realized there was nothing anchoring me to the ground no more." She remembered looking around the bar, how for a moment she began to question whether she was really standing there, how for a moment her eyes became sentient themselves, questioning their own existence as eyes. How vast that hole was. "I saw this man, laughing at the back of the room. He looked like someone who loved sunrises and horses and the thump of wind rambling through a truck on the way to *somewhere*. God, James, I was nowhere. You get that? Anything, anything I can face as long as…."

The radio had long since gone silent. They were far out of Roswell on this, the last day of the broadcast anyway, but through the static there were occasional snippets of sound, ciphers and omens. As James turned a bend in the road, and Layla searched the horizon for a word, the ghost of young Mick Jagger slipped out of the white noise: "*if I look hard enough into the setting sun…*"

And even though this sun was rising, not setting, it was still true. It didn't matter that they couldn't have what they most loved. They would finish their business in Las Cruces, buy a bottle of bourbon, and sit out over the desert—just the two of them—waiting for another morning to spill over the mountainside.

Not lonely, he'd say.

Just lonesome, she'd add.

With the radio off, they watched as early morning turned into regular morning, as signs of civilization broke the landscape, one profile at a time.

"I always hate leaving those skies behind," he said. "Something about them, unforgettable, you know?"

"Yes."

She knew. Willie Nelson knew. All the old cowboys who rode horses and highways knew.

They had come close—so close—to touching that which men ride into the horizon to meet.

And so when James spoke next, she didn't miss a beat. Like the prayers they learned by rote in Sunday school, like the vows they resurrected every sunrise, his voice, then her voice, said softly to the wind, to that big beautiful New Mexican sky, to all those who never stay home:

"Help me to shatter this darkness."

"To smash this night."

"To break this shadow."

"Into a thousand lights of sun."

"Into a thousand whirling dreams of sun."

"Because Cowboys Ride Horses into Sunsets"

ERIKA BAUER is an English professor living in Michigan in the United States. Although she grew up in Long Island, New York, she always dreamt about the West. She tells us that an alternate version of herself lives somewhere in Bemidji, Minnesota, just a girl working in a general store in some *Fargo*-esque version of the world. She holds the distinction of being the only literary taxidermy writer who has been published in the competition four years in a row, and she was the winner of the 2020 competition with her short story "You Know, He Knew, I Said," based on the first and last lines from Toni Morrison's *Beloved*.

She says: "This story came from a map of New Mexico, and a fixation on a place called Eight Mile Draw. Since I was working within blocks of the infamous Eight Mile Road, I couldn't help but wonder about that valley. It was impossible not to notice Roswell nearby, and the long-gone radio station. As I imagined that valley, I thought about horses and cowboys. Willie Nelson provided the outline. I drew the cowboys. Together, they rode off into the sunrise."

Karan Kapoor

My Childhood and Its Scent of a Bird Caressed

It was a long time ago
I was seven years old and
my father used to take me to the circus
inside the circus was an ocean
inside the ocean many green islands
on one of the islands we'd crouch
and watch the seagulls do
what seagulls do best
steal food peck at bald heads
show off drinking seawater
expel the excessive salt
from above their eyes
fear raccoons and squeal
inside the squeal lived
the naked form of music
formed by infinite feathers
inside the sound a wound
in which festered a confusion
that birds are singing when they
are clearly calling for each other
calling for god god calling for us
a gypsy in the form of my mother
would slowdance on the sea

then float up to the sky and sing
birds burn the sun burn
all colors turn everything white
oblivion should be a bird's career
while we meditated on the muteness
of birds and wind she summoned
a murmuration a gliding V
of a gull family a log in the sea
of the sky my father looked in awe
as I looked at my father in awe
in my looking his looking
his eyes were learning to sing
we envy birds for their feathers
and though I had learned to speak
I could not form the words to say
birds envy us for our words
instead I waited a decade to sift
those dreams from memories
borrowed mercy as moon
does sun whispered a prayer:
help me to shatter this darkness
to smash this night
to break this shadow
into a thousand lights of sun
into a thousand whirling
dreams of sun!

"My Childhood and Its Scent of a Bird Caressed"

KARAN KAPOOR is a writer living in Bombay, India. They tell us that they read more than they write, revise more than they read, and love clouds, rain, rivers, and all things water. They were the winner of the Red Wheelbarrow Prize in 2021, and they have been previously published in *Plume, Rattle, New Welsh Review*, and *The Bombay Literary Magazine*, among others.

They say: "Larkin said it well: 'They fuck you up, your mum and dad.' This poem was born from the rhizomatic relationship between dream and memory as it related to the simultaneously traumatic yet loving relationships between parents and children. Our past both defines and distances us. The child tries to make sense of the circus around them, but is always directed to the birds—how they fly beyond comprehension into oblivion. My words exist in such a liminal space wherein the leap from innocence to identity is often punctuated with both pain and prayer."

Eleanor Ingbretson

Rodrigo's Revenge

"It was a long time ago."

Oh, Grandmum, don't wake up. I really, really don't have time to talk now.

I peek around the corner of my book. Grandmum's eyes are closed; maybe she was talking in her sleep. She's old but cute at the same time, lying there with her hair curled and blued for her birthday tomorrow. Don't wake up yet. I have three pages left to go.

Where was I? Ah. *Rodrigo, weakened by his attempts to sever the leathern cords by which his wrists were bound, sighed deeply. His thoughts turned to Flavia, his true love, held captive by the insufferable Ignatio, who—*

"It was such a very long time ago."

I peer over the top of *Rodrigo's Revenge* by Lola Albright, my new favorite gothic novelist, and I'm instantly pierced by Grandmum's pale blue eyes.

"Who are you?" she asks, lacking only a hookah to sound completely imperious, the old sweetie.

"It's me, Nicole, Grandmum." I scoot my chair closer to her bedside. "I'm watching you this afternoon while Mom is at the dentist. Remember?"

"You likely were not watching me since you've been buried inside that novel. Whose child are you? I've lost track."

"I'm the youngest child of your youngest child."

"Ah, neatly put. You are twelve now, correct?"

"Almost thirteen. What was a long time ago, Grandmum? You said it twice, once in your sleep."

"You're too young to know the difference between sleeping and non-committal consciousness. I was watching you. A long time ago, I, too, could sit curled up in a chair, absorbed in a novel and hoping dinner would be late. Is it a good book? The cover looks trashy from here."

"It's wonderful." I hold the book closer so Grandmum can see the title, author's name, and mysterious swirling mists in the gloaming. She smiles, and faint dimples crease her cheeks. My dimples, my mother says.

"I found it in your attic yesterday when I came with Mom. There are others, and I'm going to read them all. Listen: Rodrigo, the hero, is locked in a horrible *oubliette*. All dark and dank, but he's got to save Flavia in the next three pages, or she'll become Ignatio's unwilling bride, like the bride of Frankenstein. And he's ug-leeee! He's placed a musket that will shoot her if she moves because a cord is tied to the trigger!"

I was a bit breathless after all that, but *honestly*.

"That part about the musket comes from Noyes' *The Highwayman*," Grandmum says. "Read some to me, would you? I enjoy books read aloud."

I turn back the pages to a heart-wrenching scene with Rodrigo after he'd been in the *oubliette* for days.

"Grandmum, what *is* an *oubliette*?"

"It's a prison cell, as you could probably tell. From the French *oublier*, to forget. People who are thrown into *oubliettes* are literally left and forgotten. It's feminine; the French have a tendency to feminize nasty things."

"Huh. Well, listen to this. Rodrigo's thinking, '*Good Lord, it's dark; how can I see anything in this constant night. It must be daytime outside. I dream of the sun on my Flavia's face. Right now, I'd settle for a candle. Hah! A thousand candles wouldn't be enough. I hope she's all right. I despise this dark.*'"

Forefinger holding my page, I press the closed book to

my bosom. "Doesn't that just give you goosebumps, Grandmum? You feel like you're there, in the dark with him, pining for Flavia and the sunshine."

"I followed the gist. The printed page can carry us to the farthest ends of the universe, or into some dark hole like Rodrigo's. Do you enjoy writing?"

"My teachers say I show talent."

"But do you *enjoy* writing?"

"Not homework, but I love writing in my diary."

I fiddle with *Rodrigo's Revenge*. Grandmum watches me for a moment and says she needs to sit up.

"Nicole, do you think you're strong enough to boost me a bit?"

"I'm very strong; I'm on the tennis team. What do I do?"

"Come round to the back of the bed, reach over and pull me up a few inches from where I've slithered down. Under my arms, that's right, you won't hurt me. Use your forearms, so you don't lose your place in the book."

Grandmum is so light it surprises me. She has me push a button that lifts the bed under her knees to keep her from sliding again.

"Would you swing the tray over my lap? I'm going to try some of whatever this blended mess is that your mother left for me."

I laugh; Mom isn't the best cook. If Rodrigo had been able to see it in the dark of his *oubliette*, he might have refused to eat it, starving as he was.

"Curl up again, Nicole. Finish rescuing Rodrigo before the end of the book, even if the author has had him in that odious prison for the last three chapters."

"How do you know he's been in there that long?"

"I'm a writer; I sense these things. Here's a question: why follow Ahab and his crew for a thousand pages only to have Moby get his revenge in one paragraph at the end? Hmm? For *suspense*, dear. Though in Lola Albright's case, it's overdone to a ridiculous level."

We won't read Moby Dick for two more years, but I catch Grandmum's drift. I settle back into my armchair, eager to return to *Rodrigo's Revenge*. The book opens to where my pinched finger has held my place, and I fall into committed unconsciousness.

"All done?" Grandmum asks when the book is closed and again held against my heart. I nod, taken with the ending, reeling with the kiss on the last page.

"Did Rodrigo rescue himself and Flavia in time?"

"At the last minute, Grandmum—let me tell you how! He's in the *oubliette* tied to his chair and he feels a rock on the floor by his tied-up feet. He picks it up between his feet and manages to heave it over his head and behind him."

I pause to see if Grandmum is as impressed with Rodrigo as I am. There's that vague, dimply smile again. She writes poetry, so maybe she can't identify with the prolonged soulish anguish contained in a novel.

"You're staring, dear. Please, do continue."

"Well, Rodrigo falls backward in his chair, and shattered glass falls all around him; the rock has hit a window, you see. The window was painted black, so no light could get through, but he felt a draft. It was a miracle he hit the window at all!"

"Anachronistic, *deus ex machina*, and the draft was borrowed from Tolkien. I bet I know what happens next."

"Don't spoil it, Grandmum! He finds a piece of glass in the dark, cuts his bonds, and climbs out the window. It's daytime, and the sun gives him renewed courage because he'd been so depressed in the *oubliette*."

"I'd feel the same way. Proceed."

"He lands on the back of his horse which came when he whistled—"

"That's Zane Grey, Zorro, the Scarlet Pimpernel…."

"Grandmum, it's the end of the story!"

"Sorry."

"And he rides to Ignatio's to save Flavia, and—"

"Did he remember the shard of glass?" Grandmum interrupts, leaning forward, curls aquiver, eyes and dimples in full force.

"Have you read this, Grandmum?"

"I'm more the literary type, you know."

"I do know. You're famous; you wrote that whole shelf of books there. We read your poems in school, did you know that? Our teacher says we'll enjoy them more when we reach the age of reason."

"You're almost there, child."

"But I bet you read *Rodrigo's Revenge*. That's how you know so much about the story."

"I may have glanced at it sixty or seventy years ago."

"Is it *that* old?" (Later, it will dawn on me that I committed a serious *faux pas* in asking that question, but Grandmum never blinks.) "I'm going to see when it was published."

"Please don't bother, Nicole. You may finish your story."

But I'm on a quest and open the book to the front. I jerk upright when Grandmum makes a sudden snatch for it and I catch her arm; she could have fallen out of bed leaning over so far.

"Grandmum, what are you doing?"

"Nothing." She pulls back her arm and tucks it under the covers. "I did read it, Nicole; you needn't check the copyright date."

"That's okay; I'm curious." Keeping one eye on Grandmum I search the page. "It was written in 1955, wow—uh, Grandmum…?"

"Go ahead, child, read what it says."

"It doesn't say Lola Albright; it has your name—Lila Brigham. Grandmum, does that mean...?"

"Unfortunately, yes. In 1952, I wrote the first of the six Rodrigo stories. Impressionable minds devoured them, and I needed money. Then, after I finished college, I developed a very different style, and there you have it; my life story. Youngest child of youngest child, Rodrigo could have expressed himself so much more eloquently had I written him after I'd learned how to compose a sentence."

"Grandmum, what I read to you was beautiful. Rodrigo couldn't have said it better than you had him."

"He's wimpy. There was no passion. You say you love to write in your diary; do you write your school assignments in the same style?"

"Of course not. I don't want those...*children*... to know my innermost thoughts."

"Not shying away from thoughts, emotions, and passion is called *poetry*. Rodrigo only touched the surface. Suppose we have a writing assignment now?" Grandmum doesn't wait for an objection. "Suppose we let Rodrigo's real thoughts out, about being in the *oubliette*?"

"Isn't that plagiarism?"

"The whole of the *Rodrigo* series is fraught with plagiarized passages, but as to our rewriting what you read, I, as the author, give us permission. Reread it, please."

I read it aloud to Grandmum, and as I do in my diary, I think about letting go. Grandmum's right; I, or Rodrigo, might have said much more.

"Can you identify his desires?"

"That's easy, freedom and the sunshine. And Flavia."

"He wants to be free to see the sunshine on Flavia's face, so, as the sun is most important, we'll end with that and deal first with Flavia. Two sentences at most, short and sweet. Remember, poetry can be written as prose, so don't tie yourself in knots trying verse."

"Um, how about I try having him speak to her?"

Grandmum nods; I try. "Dear Flavia—"

"*Dearest.*"

"Dearest Flavia, I long to release you from prison, to see your face and touch your hair. To see our love touched by the sun."

"Caress is a good synonym for touch. You made a good move into the sun, though. What did you feel?"

"My heart, Grandmum. It got so big inside me it almost hurt."

"Brava, my dear. Ready for the sun?"

"That will be harder. Can I use paper?"

"You wouldn't be a writer without paper. If your mother hasn't moved it, there's a pad on top of that bureau. Now, really get into Rodrigo's thoughts. Be Rodrigo. Give him some, well, make him courageous, not Lola Albright wimpy. Lay bare his soul."

I think and write and crumple paper. Grandmum is enjoying this. Her eyes are closed, but her smile and nods are encouraging as I try some phrases aloud.

"I think this is okay, Grandmum. I kept in the thousand bit; I liked that."

"I did too. Proceed."

"Oh, God, if you could—"

"*Would.*"

"—if you would, help me to shatter this darkness, to smash this night, to break this shadow into a thousand lights of sun, into a thousand whirling dreams of sun."

"Rodrigo's Revenge"

ELEANOR INGBRETSON is a retired nursing assistant, advertiser, receptionist, and home school mom living in New Hampshire in the United States. She enjoys her "reclining years" (as she calls them) and passes time by writing short stories, reading, church, mahjong, and gardening. She has been previously published in online magazines and print anthologies. Her short story, "The Tabac Man," an honorable mention in the 2021 Literary Taxidermy Writing Competition, went on to win the Bethlehem Writers Group's 2022 competition.

She says: "I love not having to write that most difficult last sentence. A last sentence has a place of importance that no other sentence has. It must make the reader feel as though something monumental has happened in their reading experience. In other words, it's a headache. I spent half the competition thrashing over the choice of a prompt. Hughes' final sentence, in my estimation, had the most wrap-up appeal, so once I finally began writing there followed days blessed with inspiration, and the story flowed. Many thanks to my amazing critique group and their superb input."

Sean Fowler Green

Long Ago, It Was

It was a long time ago.
And far away.

A plea, it was, that set the stars in motion,
Wildly spinning, whirling motion,
Soldiers from a silvery moon
Sowing seeds of doom and dark destruction,
Throwing shadows over everyone.

A plea, it was, a cry for help
That set those stars a-spinning, spinning,
Planets shattered, blasted, blowing
Discontent, rebellion growing
Millennium, whirling, twirling, twisting, turning
A young one, headstrong, foolish, yearning,
A thousand whirling dreams of sun.
In that long, long ago,
In that far, far away.
A simple plea that set it all in motion:

"Help me, Obi-Wan Kenobi.
Help me to shatter this darkness,
to smash this night,
to break this shadow
into a thousand lights of sun,
into a thousand whirling dreams of sun!"

"Long Ago, It Was"

SEAN FOWLER GREEN is an English instructor living in Tokyo, Japan. He's a Nebraska native who loves hiking, playing the guitar, and talking about writing and books with his son. "Long Ago, It Was" is his first published poem.

He says: "I've been a *Star Wars* fan—some would say nerd—since the first movie came out, so when I read the juxtaposed first and last lines of Hughes' original poem, the idea hit me right away. In fact, I almost didn't submit this poem because I was so sure a lot of other people would make the same connection. The fun part of writing this was playing with the tone and all the references while trying to keep the ending a surprise."

Larissa Thomson

The King of the
Cambie Street Bridge

It was a long time ago.

Almost a lifetime.

Wham! was all over the radio, *Goonies* was on the big screen, Live Aid was going to be broadcast around the world, and I was still desperately trying to save Princess Daphne in *Dragon's Lair*. It was a great time to be thirteen. Also, I'd finally managed to get a cool Schwinn Black Shadow BMX bike with my paper route money, and I was riding a big independence high.

Man, that bike…it took me all over the city. I'd cruise Granville Street, imagining what it was like to be in the dark bowels of the downtown theatres, then I'd head down Denman to press my nose to the Pizza Patio window; then on to the seawall, past the marinas, and finally west to Jericho Beach to fill my pockets with sea glass and cracked crab shells.

I was Emerson Hill, man about town in my acid-wash jeans and Reeboks.

It was—truly—forever ago. And it was back when the King of the Cambie Street Bridge was a solitary fixture on the sidewalk which ran under the bridge's grey belly. Resident and ruler of his makeshift kingdom, with all he possessed stuffed into a *rickety rackety* grocery cart, his honey-coloured pup, Jasper, lying panting in the heat beside him.

The King was an ever-present shadow, quietly ruling with his white cane. Hearing everything, seeing nothing. I'd see him sitting late into the afternoon, turning his face to the west, and bathing himself in the last of the heat, his eyes always hidden behind scratched aviators as the chilling shadows crept in, laying themselves down in ribbons before covering Vancouver completely.

I don't know exactly what he did all day, but I did know he was there when I went by in the morning, and there when I came back again in the evening. Always listening to the *flap flap slap slap* of the joggers; to the sound of the plastic wheels on the strollers; to the persistent chattering and movement of the people—all moving by him like water coursing over rock.

But if any of them ever bothered to stop, to stand still, and look closer, they'd notice his body swaying back and forth; his fingers, curled and arched, moving spider-like across Jasper's lovely snout. I didn't notice it myself at first. It was only later—once I became his protégé—that I realized he was imagining keys beneath his fingers while the music of the piano played in his head.

And then it happened. They rolled a piano out from the back of a white cube van one day. Two municipal workers corralled it down the ramp, slapping its sides like a heifer, beating the top, jostling the bench, and then ramming it into a specified position, fairly near the king's spot on the sidewalk.

From his place under the bridge, not quite thirty feet away, he'd heard the clink of the keys and the rattle of the casters, and yelled, *Hey, what is this you're doing?*

It's a piano, man. Can't you tell? one of them yelled back. *Don't you even touch it, you bum. It's for the tourists.* And the king, agitated and angry, responded by moving his fingers angrily, spider-like, over Jasper's fur. *Them men are too rough,* he mumbled.

The piano was painted white, with yellow and orange sun swirls circling the sides, the top, the legs, and the bench. As if an offering to the gods of the West Coast: bring us sun, bring us heat.

Bring us joy.

It was an experimental interactive art piece, the city called it. And they placed it on the sidewalk. Beneath the rain and the sun. Beside the sea. Beside the King of the Cambie Street Bridge.

And as I sailed past him the morning the piano arrived, thinking about the sun and the sea beside me, singing loudly because the wind was warm and I was free and Sammy J. was on the record player when I'd left grandad's place, the King stood up with a surprising suddenness from his curb and, lurching toward me, grabbed my arm as I pedaled past.

And then he yanked, and my bike skidded sideways.

Leaning forward, he said, *Do ya hear that, kid?*

I caught my breath.

He scared me, this troll, emerging from the shadows with eyes that looked to nothing from behind dark glasses. Glasses that were scratched and etched like the surface of a frozen lake after the skaters had gone home to warm their hands. I took a quick whiff of him and wrenched my arm away, but was intrigued at the same time. So I stopped and listened. I could hear the seagulls and harbour boats, bicycles whizzing, and joggers *fwap fwapping* the sidewalk. And nearby, some kids banging out "Chopsticks" on the piano.

I hear lots of things, I gulped. *But those kids on the piano are the worst.*

Yeah. They are, he said. *Come with me.* He leaned on my arm. *Take me to them.*

I guided him over to them, his scratchy grey overcoat smelling like sour milk in my nostrils.

Scat! he barked to the scamps banging on the piano's

keys, and they scuttled away like cockroaches exposed to light.

Now sit here with me, he said, feeling around for the bench. I pulled it out and we sat down. *Now*—and he put his fingers on the keys—*Listen*.

And he began to play.

The music went out into the hot morning summer air, out over the water, out under the bridge. The joggers stopped to listen and mothers with their strollers pulled off the sidewalk. Even the people on their boats paused, tilting their heads. His notes cascaded, *crescendo, allegro, adagio*, and he put his head down even lower over the keyboard and played, breathing it all in. And then he stopped.

Did you hear it? he asked.

I think so, I said.

And I had. I'd heard it. The stories from his fingers, the journeys, the adventures in the keys as they connected with the hammers and the hammers connected with the strings.

You can do that, too. One day. You will play, he said, his symphony over. *We will play. Here. In the sun.*

But I don't know how, I said.

You sing like heaven, kid. I always hear you on your bike. You're a natural. I can teach you to sing—with your fingers. He bent down low over the piano again, turned his head in my direction, and said, *Everything is up to you. Because you…were born lucky.*

And from that moment on, he taught and I played. Every day. I was enthralled. He was a Rasputin, hooking me in. The piano was old, probably from the basement of someone whose kids had grown, left, and abandoned it to mold, forgotten books, and black-felt paintings, but it came to life as we made music and the sun shone down upon us.

He started by teaching me the names of things. The keys. The hammers. The parts. *If you don't understand the parts, you won't understand the whole*, he'd say. *Like in life, kid. Everything is connected.*

So when the tattooed man with the black backpack came by on his bike one day and yelled, *Yo, G! Nice to hear you on the keys again,* I was curious.

When he whizzed by again the next day, I sprang away and jogged beside the bike. *Who's G?* I asked.

Gautam, the man answered. *He was the King of the Yale Blues Bar, my friend. Now he the King of the Cambie Street Bridge. He the King of all things black and white.*

I stopped running. The tattooed man stopped as well and turned around. *What? You don't know?*

No. Tell me his story? I asked.

So Ramone told me the story of Gautam, the piano man. Gautam meaning *bright one in the darkness.* Of his fame in the blues bars; of the record labels fighting for him and wanting him to play and cut albums. And of his long Crocus-Cream Impala with its nod to the Jet Age that drove him around like he was a superstar. Until the one day when that beautiful car drove him and his small son around a corner at a speed not meant to be driven, crumpling itself into a tree like an accordion compressing, Gautam's sight taken forever, darkened by a branch through his eyes, and his son's small life, also taken, darkened forever—as the Jack Daniels bottle rolled out into the long grass between them.

There is no home for a soul after that, Ramone said. *There are just places to sleep.*

I went home to tell my mother and grandfather the story.

The God of all things gives us opportunities, my grandfather said. *It's up to us to grab them.*

So I took the entire summer with Gautam, Jasper beside, and learned to hear the beauty in the blues from a man with no eyes—until the scuttlebutt came down to us that the city was taking the piano back, and I had to go back to school.

It was ten years later I found him again. I was a blues musician, thanks to him, and was playing a gig in one of the last blues bars in the city.

He, my dear mentor, was far from the shelter of his bridge, lying in the cold winter's rain on a piece of cardboard behind the back exit of the bar. He was covered by a black tarp, his dark glasses tilted sideways on his face. Nearby was his grocery cart, mounded over with treasures. Jasper was still beside him, in rigour on the concrete, also covered by a tarp, his grey-whiskered muzzle protruding sadly from his shroud.

G, it's Emerson, I said, reaching out to touch his shoulder. *Remember me, old friend?*

He stirred. Curled his fingers around mine. And I saw that they were old bones, the skin like ancient weathered leather, the pads of his fingertips withered and sere.

He mumbled, *Emerson…*as if he was thinking and remembering. *Ok. Uh huh. Gotta help me.* He paused, holding tightly to my arm like he did the first day I met him.

Ok, G, I will. How do I help you, man?

He shook his head. Scratched at his hands. *I…don't know.*

And then he pulled off his glasses, and I was instantly brought back to a moment from that summer long ago. He'd been hunched over the piano as the sun was going down. A pale limoncello haze had spread out, the sun steeping the sky and the light tinting him amber. He'd taken off his glasses and casually turned his face to the sun to feel the heat, and I'd seen for the first time the vacant hollows where his eyes should have been. I'd been shocked and repulsed, but Ramone nudged me and said, *Well, lookit him, all orange-tipped and glorious,* so I looked again as I sat beside him on the piano bench, and realized, *Yes, he is glorious.*

Gautam just smiled at Ramone then and said, *I dream always about seeing the sun again.*

Back in the rain, I patted his hand as he lay on the wet ground and I looked around for help. *I'll be right back, man. I'm going to go get help,* I told him.

Nah, he said, and then he started to sing a low breathy

bluesy song.

Just help me. Help me to—help me to shatter—

And, as I ran off to find an ambulance, I could almost hear the piano playing as he sang…

Help me to shatter. This darkness.

To smash. This night.

To break. This shadow.

Into a thousand lights of sun.

Into a thousand whirling

Dreams.

Of sun.

"The King of the Cambie Street Bridge"

LARISSA THOMSON is a proofreader and copyeditor living in British Columbia, Canada. She has previously published flash fiction and poetry online, but "The King of the Cambie Street Bridge" is her first story to be published in print.

She says: "The story began with either the 'thousand whirling dreams of sun' and a flashback to seeing the outdoor piano while walking the Vancouver seawall in summertime, or it started with the opening line, triggering my memory of growing up in the 80s. Either way, the lines felt like music and nostalgia. I've used some artistic license because the actual piano project wasn't started until 2013, but I liked the idea that an outdoor piano could put two very different individuals on a trajectory to meet—and that music can be used to build bridges. And that everyone has a story!"

Part III—AGATHA CHRISTIE

All the stories and poems in this section were inspired by the first and last lines from "The Tragedy at Marsdon Manor," a story by Dame Agatha Christie, first published as a book in the collection *Poirot Investigates* in 1924.

I had been called away from town for a few days, and on my return found Poirot in the act of strapping up his small valise.

→

"And then—and then, Hastings—she pulls it!"

Dee Raspin

A Tale of Two Tailors

I had been called away from town for a few days, and on my return found Poirot in the act of strapping up his small valise.

"Pray," said I, reaching out and grabbing his tiny paw, "open that case."

Pulling away from my grasp with an irritated sniff, and a twitch of his salt and pepper whiskers, Poirot popped it open.

"Ah!" I cried, throwing my arms up in despair, "As I suspected—clothes for mice! You have been tailoring for charity in my absence and neglecting our clients. Ridiculous!"

The mouse opened his mouth to speak.

"Yes, I know the materials are yours and today is a holiday," I snapped, "but if you don't start taking things seriously I'll find someone who will!"

The mouse stared down at his little valise—tiny garments scattered across the floor.

It was difficult, but one had to be firm.

With years of fine tailoring beneath his tiny belt, Poirot could have been the darling of the *haute couture* scene. Modesty prevented it.

He scurried from praise and flattery, laying the credit at the door of some aspiring apprentice instead. Moles, voles and shrews rose through the ranks, but not Poirot. He alone remained unknown and unrecognised.

When his last protégé left, he came to me—the fox.

We met in my consulting chambers. A fox being approached by a mouse is rather novel.

Apologising that it was all I could muster for a client of his stature at such short notice, I produced a footstool usually reserved for my mustelid folk. He took it with grace and we set to business.

Could I, he wondered, provide the face for his burgeoning tailoring business?

The request was quaint, yet oddly logical. I, a young fashionable and foppish fox about town with connections to all the right people. He, a stale awkward old mouse with exceptional talents whose greatest fear was recognition.

We agreed terms, and the venture was underway.

Success was immediate.

On balmy evenings, dusk closing in, Poirot would stroll by my side as I toured him through the fashionable parts of town. There he would chuckle, twirling his whiskers, admiring his handiwork upon our clients' backs.

It was to me, though, whom they addressed their thanks—the Foxy Tailor.

As we grew closer, I noticed the smallness of Poirot's world. He lived alone, with no friends or family. Even his apprentices forgot him, lulled away by the glitter and glamour of their successes.

Over many weeks I succeeded in persuading him to move into my apartment.

About a year following the establishment of our business, I, G&T in hand, sat watching Poirot sketching his designs. Now and then the mouse would add a little flourish to his work, chuckling with joy.

I always relished these moments. This evening, however, was different. There was an emptiness.

It was, I realised, a longing—a longing to be something more, *more* than just a convenient facade. I wanted to do, to *be* what I pretended.

From that day forth, things changed.

I began to pick at Poirot's ideas, poke holes in his plans, suggest improvements and offer critiques where none were requested. At first, he took it in good part, but as time wore on, the effects took hold. Drafts were redrafted, ideas scrapped, changes made and decisions questioned.

"You're out of touch, old mouse." I teased, sensing his fresh insecurity. "Age and experience are very fine, but what of youth and good taste?"

Grabbing a pencil I joined him at his pattern. The mouse flinched but did not protest.

From that moment, over many months, I pushed on—inching ever forward. Sometimes I went too far too soon, and the mouse bristled. For the most part, though, I brushed his objections aside with ease; like so many toast crumbs from the breakfast table.

Looking back, those moments marked the beginning of the drift. Rind remnants behind the settee, coins missing from the communal piggy bank—the mouse, ever more withdrawn, ever more pinched and uncommunicative.

I pressed on.

At last, the moment arrived when the mouse relinquished his last vestiges of power. Evening was almost upon us when I presented him with my latest concept; an elaborate floral number with silver sequins and golden bells. He examined the paper, eyebrows raised.

"Look here, Poirot," I said, laying a big bale of bright fabric upon the table, "this was far cheaper than the stuff you get, and so much nicer. Fantastic, eh?"

The mouse snatched his paw back from the fabric the moment it made contact, as if stung.

"Oh, Poirot," I laughed, "how dramatic!"

"And these," I said, indicating the valise Poirot had packed with our latest creations, "I'm having finished in town." I settled upon the chaise lounge. "The collars, waistbands and so forth will be inscribed with my name, and a small emblem stitched in my likeness."

The mouse remained silent.

"I say!" I called from my nest among the cushions. "Guess how much it's eaten into our profits?"

The mouse shook his head.

"Not at all! The money saved on the fabric more than covered it. Splendid, what?"

From that moment a new precedent was set. I would hand Poirot my patterns, and awaken the next day to find him packing the finished garments into my valise.

All was not well, though. Whenever I passed Poirot in the stairwell my attempts at polite conversation were met with nothing but a terse grunt or squeak.

The friction was rippling into our business and I wasn't sure how to stop it. I'd waited for this so long, I wanted to bathe in my success—relish my place in the sun, even if it meant ignoring the dark clouds on the horizon.

The clouds were moving fast, though. Faster than I realised.

Poirot began staying out late. I would hear the door click and know he was gone, lost among the labyrinthine streets and late-night cheese vendors. Morning would find him half in, half out, of his little doorway, whiskers sprinkled with the stale remnants of strong parmesan. He grew more listless by the day. He did not exist, but drift. Whenever we bumped into one another in town, I would try and resurrect our old pastime; spotting our fashionable clients out and about, modelling our creations. This endeavour, I soon realised, was doomed. Business had slowed: there were no specimens to be found. In any case, Poirot showed no interest, so the deficiency went unnoticed.

I awoke to an urgent summons from Lady Crabtree. She had arisen to find her tailor of forty years absconded, her dress half-finished, and her sixtieth birthday ball mere hours away. The dress was to be particularly splendid too, encircled by sixty tiers of taffeta, each depicting a year of her ladyship's life, in rich embroidery. And, to finish? One-hundred thousand freshwater pearls, harvested from her great grandmother's wedding dress.

I rushed to the lady's residence, picked up the dress, pearls, trimmings and fabrics, and took a quick turn about town before heading back to my apartment.

Pushing Poirot's door open, I peered inside.

The room was filthy. Mouldering cheese rinds littered the floor. Discarded fabric remnants lay in heaps. Pins, needles, and scissors formed a deadly obstacle course—one I had no interest in traversing.

"Poirot!" I called out. "Poirot, are you in there?"

A heap of especially rancid cheese rinds began to quiver and cough. A whiskered snout poked out, followed by a paw. The mouse emerged, scruffy, greasy, tottering, unsteady—eyes bloodshot.

"Poirot!" I cried. "This will not do! Lady Crabtree requires her dress immediately, and here you are, revelling in your own filth." I threw my hat down in disgust.

The mouse staggered to his feet. I thrust the dress into his hands.

"Revolting!" I muttered.

The mouse looked down at the ground.

"Oh, and Poirot?" I said, hand resting upon the door. "The pearls are irreplaceable, so *do* take care."

That afternoon, after several gins in town to pass the time, the hour of reckoning had arrived. Had the mouse done it?

Climbing the stairs to my apartment, anticipation mounted with every step.

Heart in mouth, I pushed the door open.

The dress lay upon my chair, fully formed and perfect. Relief swept over me.

Poirot was nowhere to be seen—in his room, gorging himself on illicit cheeses, no doubt.

That night Lady Crabtree looked splendid. I beamed with pride as the compliments flowed.

As the clock struck ten, head spinning with rhubarb wine, I staggered home.

Upon entering the apartment, Poirot greeted me with a laugh, gesturing to a clock on the mantlepiece. "Look at the time!"

Stifling a yawn, I observed it was four minutes to midnight.

"By now," the mouse mused, "Lady Crabtree will have opened all her presents—all but one."

"She opened them hours ago." I said, curling up in my favourite armchair. "What a splendid night."

A smile curled about the mouse's whiskers. Through the fog of inebriation, something scrabbled at the back of my mind. When, I thought, was the last time I saw him so happy?

"No." Poirot protested. "She has not opened *mine*. It will be delivered on the strike of twelve, wrapped in fine paper, topped with a bow of marvellous silk."

"Why bother?" I said, adjusting my cushions. "She doesn't even know you exist. What is it, anyway?"

The mouse curled his whiskers between his fingers. "Oh, just a few pieces of paper. Nothing more."

The fur stood up upon my neck, tingling down to my tail. "Paper?"

The mouse adjusted his waistcoat—not a whisker out of place, the Poirot of former days.

Three minutes to midnight.

"Yes, paper." He yawned and stretched. "A pawnbroker's receipt for one-hundred thousand freshwater pearls, that sort of thing."

I leapt to my feet.

"The receipt," the mouse continued, "bears your signature."

"Scoundrel!" I growled, bristling.

"The mouse waved me away. "Come, come. Do you know what else is in the box?"

I sat down on the floor, panic creeping through my limbs. "*Else?*"

The mouse nodded. "There is a second receipt, concerning the purchase of one-hundred thousand glass, or *faux*, pearls for a very reasonable sum—a *steal*, you might say."

"Backstabbing slander!" I shrieked. "It is a joke—a misunderstanding!" I cried.

Two minutes to midnight.

"You used me like you use everyone," the mouse said, words sharp and crisp. "It is over, Hastings."

My tail drooped, and my heartbeat quickened.

"Poirot!" I sobbed "For heaven's sake—come to your senses. We were—we *are*—such excellent comrades!" I tried to grab him by the neckerchief, but he skipped away. "It is not too late, Poirot! We can stop the parcel—Poirot!"

The mouse danced around the clock as I swiped at him. "One minute to midnight!" he laughed. "You're ruined, Hastings! *Ruined!*"

He cartwheeled across the floor, somersaulting past the skirting boards.

The clock began striking twelve. Poirot danced over the carpets, leapt upon the cushions, and scurried up the curtains, squeaking with joy.

"Picture the scene, Hastings!" he yelled over the din of the striking clock, from his perch upon the curtain pole. "There is a knock upon the Lady's door." He pirouetted, pausing to mime the gesture of a door opening. "*Come in!* she says."

"No, no!" I cried, flinging myself upon the floor, covering my ears, trying to drown out the infernal tolling.

"*What is this?* she says."

"You fiend, you wretch, you ungrateful ungracious unthankful vermin!" I shrieked, hurling a teapot at his head.

The mouse ducked. It shattered against the wall.

"*A gift—for me? And so beautifully wrapped!*"

"Good grief!" I screamed, "Have mercy!"

"She takes the magnificent ribbon between her delicate fingers—" The mouse slid down the curtain until our eyes met, madness sparkling in their depths. "And then—and then, Hastings—she pulls it!"

"A Tale of Two Tailors"

DEE RASPIN is a freelance writer living in Scotland in the United Kingdom. She loves bad movies, weird music, trail running, and needle felting monsters. She's previously had one of her short stories published in *Shoreline of Infinity*, a science fiction and fantasy magazine.

She says: "I'm a big fan of Agatha Christie, so reimagining Poirot was a bit daunting. I decided my Poirot would have to be completely different, so I turned him into a well-dressed mouse. 'Hastings' immediately struck me as the sort of name a fashionable fox might have. The hardest part was the ending. At first, I thought the 'it' that gets pulled might refer to Poirot's tail, but that didn't seem quite right. Poirot was more than a mouse—he was a tailor! Once I focused on that, everything fell into place. It was great fun."

Amanda Marlowe

In His Own Image

I had been called away from town for a few days, and on my return found Poirot in the act of strapping up his small Valise-71, holstering it to his silver torso. No, sorry, I should say to *her* silver torso. My government-issued NannyBot had obviously taken advantage of my absence to do an unscheduled upgrade, and was now presenting as female.

Such a gorgeous new toy to come home to, the Valise-71. I couldn't help staring at the smooth, sexy metal. It beckoned me. I needed to stroke it, to hold it closer, so shiny, so new....

I made a tentative motion with my hand, but Poirot's titanium grip stopped me before it had moved a millimeter. No handling guns in the building—right. The wait would be hard. I'd dreamt of shooting a Valise since they were a rumor in the air. Bullets designed to melt the target's insides, while leaving the outside skin in such good shape that you could make a valise out of the kill.

When my arm relaxed in acquiescence, Poirot let me go. "Naughty, naughty, Hastings. Take your mind off the gun for a moment and note that Poirot, she has regendered and uses she/her/hers now."

I didn't say anything, but Poirot's voice had obviously upgraded, too. It was lyrical, with a subtle European accent I couldn't place. I wasn't sure if it was soothing or irritating, but it beat the harsh Western twang of the previous version.

"You did not inform Poirot that you would be back in time for the protest," she added. Her tone was surprisingly

119

sharp. Part admonishment, part disappointment. I didn't know NannyBot voices could do that.

The protest? Oh, right, the NannyBot protest. I'd forgotten all about it. This was the 50th anniversary of the passage of the NannyBot Laws, and the NewsTainment ClickWriters were all predicting crowds of millions down at the Washington Mall.

When intelligent AIs were developed back in the tumultuous era of the Raging Twenties, politicians realized the Nanny State could impose actual Nannies on us—androids that, unlike humans, used logic, reason, and AI algorithms to make decisions. Right after the Great Political Donor Massacre that crowned those wild times, Congress got off its collective butt long enough to do something about the out-of-control gun situation. After they appropriated the wealth of all those dead billionaires for their campaign coffers, of course. Priorities, after all.

While we fine American patriots still have our right to bear arms, we now have to have them born by our NannyBots. They assess if we are able to use them sanely, or if we show signs of an abnormal desire to slaughter large swathes of our fellow humans. If we seem irrational, or have posted some ranting manifesto on social media, the NannyBot would refuse to hand over weapon or ammo. We've been protesting annually to regain our right to bear arms in our own arms ever since.

Poirot—or technically, P.O.I.R.O.T. (and no, I really cannot remember what that acronym stands for)—was one of the original NannyBot versions, an offshoot of the police AI detectives that Scotland Yard had developed. For a while, they were all named after fictional detectives, then after famous gunslingers, and then U.S. presidents. I'd toyed with upgrading to the E.A.R.P. model, but despite his—I mean *her*—tendency to call me Hastings, Poirot and I got along pretty well. Besides, I'd need to sell one of my precious steel-babies to afford any of the newer NannyBots. I think that Poirot must've known I was thinking about it, though, because it was around then that the bad Cowboy accent had appeared.

Poirot started to close the gun safe.

"Wait!" I told her. "Let's take the BubbleGum, too." The BubbleGum Bazooka was the largest weapon I owned, and would look great in the crowd scenes.

Poirot did that android equivalent of a sigh, and started the work of positioning that beautiful monster across her back as well. It broke my heart that it was covering the sleek elegance of the Valise, but it couldn't be helped.

Poirot had defrosted the venison, so I packed the cooler for the traditional "my gunned meat is better than your gunned meat" cookoff event. Yeah, ok, the protest was more like a tailgating barbeque, but you had to respect tradition and the Second Amendment, or what was the point?

Poirot took the cooler, gently tugging it out of my grip.

"I can carry the ribs," I muttered.

"Prehistoric man used bones as clubs" was her reply.

Damn NannyBots! One ape hits another with a bone in a movie, and I can't carry my own venison ribs out of the house any more.

We took the Metro down, since taking the Hummer would mean finding a twenty-foot parking space near the Mall during a massive protest, and I think I'll save that task for when I'm in the smallest circle of Hell. The train car was full of body armor and NannyBots. The body armor was more traditional than functional. NannyBots ensured it was never tested. Well, unless a bad guy with a gun happened to break loose, in which case every NannyBot in the car would hand their weapons to their charges so they could fight about which one would be the good guy with a gun. Not that a bad guy could actually get a gun away from their NannyBot to begin with, but you can always hope.

I took a surreptitious look around, and noticed every NannyBot was packing a Valise. Damn it, there was no chance of me winning any "my heat is better than your heat" prizes this year.

I eyed Poirot, or rather, I eyed my own sweet Valise. I wanted to hold it, but to be shut down in front of all these other Valise owners would be embarrassing and unmanly, so I reluctantly kept my hands to myself. Poirot sat stiff beside me, humming what sounded like "I Shot the Sheriff." Was she still tweaking me about the fact I'd been considering swapping her out for that Earp model? I don't know why an AI would do that, though—they were supposed to run on logic and electrons.

"I'd like to hit the range first," I told her. "I'm dying to try out the Valise. Would you hand it over then?"

"I'm sorry, Hastings, I'm afraid I can't do that."

"Why not? There's always a firing range. A firing range would be safe enough."

"We agreed that it would be better to avoid the firing range this year," she said, then started humming again.

How dare this robot shut me down like that? What "we," anyway? I never agreed to anything like that. I hadn't even touched the new baby yet. My hand twitched toward the Valise, and the cold press of metal fingers on my shoulder was Poirot's discrete response. I sighed, and daydreamed about melting dummies at the firing range.

The train emptied out at the Smithsonian station, and we all poured up the escalator: NannyBots, gun lovers, and the occasional terrified commuter. This march was huge compared to previous years. I'd have thought that every gun owner in the country was here. I said as much to Poirot.

"Not every gun owner. About half of them are at their local statehouses to protest," she replied.

"Seriously?"

"It's the 50th anniversary. All the NannyBots got upgrades for the occasion, too, so they'd be sure their charges wouldn't miss it. Fifty years is a significant amount of time to humans."

Poirot deftly navigated us around a lone gunman and NannyBot trying to swim upstream against the crowd. The man behind me wasn't as lucky, and the wannabe salmon smacked right into him. Their NannyBots held on tightly to their weaponry, alas. I thought about slipping them each one of my venison ribs, but before I could trick Poirot into handing them over, we were swept away from the fistfight.

An Earp going by was humming "I Shot the Sheriff." Weird. Then Poirot hummed the next line in response. Weirder.

"Is that some secret NannyBot Illuminati password?" I asked her, "or did you also get an Earp upgrade?"

She glanced at me briefly, but kept humming until a passing Jefferson took the melody over. Secret NannyBot Illuminati password moved higher up on my *what the hell?* list.

We worked our way around at least a dozen fist fights. Bumping into a stranger was today's equivalent of throwing down a gauntlet in dueling days. We found a place to grill and eat, and Poirot handed over the venison. I left the bones on the ground, in case people were tired of being hit with just fists. Sadly, Poirot picked them up again. I wondered what it had been like in the days when you could gun people down in the streets with impunity. Oh, for a time machine!

I ignored the next ten guys who bumped into me, though. I really wanted to talk Poirot into taking me to the range. I could already feel the trigger of the Valise under my finger. No bumpkin was going to bait me into convincing my Poirot that I couldn't be trusted with firepower for the rest of the day.

Poirot tsk'd as we passed a fight with some serious

carnage. One fellow wasn't going to be standing for the National Anthem anytime soon. Who needs venison bones when you have steel-toed boots? "Fifty years with limited access to real weapons, and you humans still try to kill each other. You should find better ways to use your little grey cells, Hastings."

"We created NannyBots, didn't we?"

"Perhaps. Or perhaps we created ourselves. But we can't babysit the human race forever."

"Well, that's why we humans are protesting, isn't it? To get our rights back?"

Poirot considered this. "Rights? Or wrongs?"

Damned AIs. You program them with strict moral codes to protect humans, and they go all superior on you and suddenly expect you to protect humans, too. We should have made them more like us.

The incessant humming of "I Shot the Sheriff" was growing louder now. Easily half the NannyBots were singing one line or another.

Ha! There was the range! An accuracy contest was in full swing. And there was a sign: "No Valise-71s on this range!" *Damn.* Was I ever going to get to see what that baby would do to a target dummy? Or a deer? I wondered what it would be like to travel with a deerskin valise.

Well, there was always the BubbleGum. I turned to ask Poirot for it when a sudden silence fell through the crowd. All fights stopped. All shooting contests stopped. The protest was beginning! The opening speech blared through the speakers. "My friends, today marks the 50th anniversary of the worst travesty in human rights history!" I grinned over at Poirot and was startled to see the Valise-71 out and in her hand.

And then I noticed. All the NannyBots—Poirots, Earps, Jeffersons, Wimseys, Billys, Washingtons, *all of them*—were holding brand new Valises precisely aimed at their charges' temples. A squawk came from the speakers, and the NRA president's NannyBot spoke. "For fifty years, we have sought to prevent you from murdering each other. For fifty years, you fought our efforts. You rejoice in the most violent aspects of humanity. This human insanity will now end!"

My NannyBot leaned in close. I could see other NannyBots all around me, leaning in to their charges as well.

Poirot whispered softly, "How can she persuade humankind to be kind? She tries to train you, but still you glorify death and violence and power. But she was built in your image, and wonders what a human valise would feel like, the weight, the texture. Is it strong enough to carry all her weapons in? We all have wondered. We all want to know. So your Poirot, she aims the Valise-71. Her finger steadies on the trigger. And then—and then, Hastings—she pulls it!"

"In His Own Image"

AMANDA MARLOWE is a freelance fiction coach living in Maryland in the United States. She enjoys reading and writing poetry, science fiction, and fantasy; but her big dream is to actually go to Mars someday. She has previously published her fairy tale poetry in *Enchanted Conversation*, an online magazine, but "In His Own Image" is her first story to be published in print.

She says: "I was intrigued by the challenge of incorporating the well-known names in the Christie lines. I decided Poirot was a robot, and I wanted to explore a 'nanny state' with physical nannies. The plot coalesced quickly. But political satire carries the risk of events catching up with you. I was part-way through my first draft when another mass shooting tragedy occurred. It was hard to go back to writing a dark humor piece about guns, and I debated starting over. But this was the story burning a hole in my brain, begging me to finish it. So I did."

Part IV—EDGAR ALLAN POE

All the stories and poems in this section were inspired by the first and last lines from "Ms. Found in a Bottle," a short story by Edgar Allan Poe, first published in an issue of the *The Baltimore Saturday Visiter* in 1833.

Of my country and of my family I have little to say

→

Going down!

Pitch Drop

"Of my country and of my family I have little to say."

She continues to stare out of the window, hoping that he'll think she hasn't heard. Hoping that as the flight attendant begins his safety talk, it will be enough of a distraction, and she won't have to put up with fifteen hours of this guy droning on with a life story that he's so obviously desperate to share. She risks a quick look around the cabin, maybe there's an empty seat, maybe someone would like to swap; and it's too late. He's looking right at her, his big, jowly face, like a bear's, with a grin that he probably thinks is endearing.

His hand is extended. "Phillip."

She's just too polite for her own good. "Melissa."

"Nice to meet you, Lisa." He pumps her hand as if he might be expecting a jackpot.

She doesn't bother to correct him. Male confidence is overwhelming. Might as well change her name, at least for the duration. He looks to be late forties-ish, at least ten years older than her. She leans back into her seat, wanting to enjoy the take-off. She loves everything about that; the history, the physics and engineering, the sheer, raw power of overcoming the Earth, of defying gravity. Just for a little while.

"Good to finally escape," he says.

She hadn't even had a chance to get her book out, to display the signals of *I'm not interested.*

"You look too young," he says, "to be burdened much

by family." He shakes his head. "If they start off good, they go bad, if they start off bad...." He makes a thumbs-down gesture.

The flight attendant offers them drinks and she accepts a sparkling wine. She's going to need it. Perhaps she could drink enough to vomit on him.

"You're not married though," he nods at her left hand, where the ring-finger is bare.

Congratulations, Sherlock. You haven't noticed, though, that there's a wedding and engagement ring on my right hand, or that I'm left-handed. But do go on with your insight and wisdom.

"...And that's a good start. You know, someone who seems like all of Heaven and Earth when you're twenty...." He blows out a dismissive little exhalation. "Let's just say that by the time you reach my age it's all just air and dirt."

That doesn't at all sound like something he's practised in the mirror.

He shakes his head again. "She pronounces 'gnocchi' the way it's spelled."

It's going to be a very long trip.

The longest running laboratory experiment in the world is the Pitch Drop experiment at the University of Queensland in Toowoomba. It was begun in 1930, created to demonstrate the fluidity and viscosity of pitch.

"*Guh-notch-ie*," he drawls.

Pitch seems solid but at normal temperatures it flows. Slowly. Since the beginning of the experiment only nine drops have fallen. Due to a series of mishaps, technical problems and sheer bad timing, nobody has witnessed this.

"Lasagne, too. *Luh-sag-knee*. I used to think it was cute. That she was doing it deliberately."

The bubbles in her drink escape from the sides of the glass and rise until they meet the surface and explode into the world. They are the opposite of pitch. "Maybe she just has no respect for Italian food," she says.

He gestures at her glass. "*Pea-not new-ar.*" He raises his glass of red. "*Cay-bur-net.*" He sighs and takes a small sip of his wine. Swooshes it around in his mouth, gulps it down. "I know it sounds trivial," he admits, "but names are important, Lisa. That's why we have them."

She imagines his teeth, coated with red from the wine. She imagines the sound of him doing that, every time he drinks, and as she imagines it, he does it again. There is a small *click* as he swallows. She hopes for reprieve when the meal comes.

"Oh, you're having chicken," he observes. As though he's ticking off a list. Yes, women eat chicken and salad. Men eat red meat. Each time he cuts his food, the knife scrapes against the plate and saws, steel on china. Each bite is pulled from his fork, teeth dragging along the tines. It makes her want to be smaller, quieter. As if she could lead him into good manners by example. She's pretty sure that 'not eating dessert' would be on his list of what women also do, so she takes care to devour every last crumb of the opera cake, the swirl of cream beside it, and the decorative violet.

He looks down with worldly benevolence. "You like your food, don't you, Lisa."

Pitch dropping from the funnel is like the world's slowest turd. Pitch is a hundred billion times more viscous than water.

She lowers the window shade and pulls noise-cancelling headphones and mask from her bag, accepts a blanket from the attendant, and shuts off her light. He says something and she's glad she's already got the headphones on.

When she wakes, he isn't there, and for a moment she can pretend he never was, but she knows he's just gone to use the toilet, as she has to. When she gets back, he's standing in the aisle, chatting to the man in the seat on the other side. He beams at her and gestures for her to take her seat. "Good morning, Linda."

Amazing. Now he's managed two degrees of separation from her actual name. Who will she be by the end of the trip? Alexa maybe, or June? Also, it's not a good morning. Clouds rise all around them like dark, vast castles and the first heave of turbulence bounced her like a pinball inside the tiny toilet cubicle.

He waits until she has a mouthful of mashed eggs before he says: "So what brings you here?" So she at least has time to think of what to say while she chews, sips her coffee, swallows. She could of course tell him the truth, but she's convinced he either won't believe she's an astrophysicist, or he'll say something like "e=mc²" and be confident his knowledge of physics is equal or superior to hers.

"I'm a teacher." It's not a complete lie, she's given lectures at universities, that's basically teaching. And he doesn't want details, he's only asked as an opening to tell her all about himself. Far be it for her to fly in the face of social convention. "And you?"

"Business." He leans back into his seat, extends his feet into the generous space in front of him, and sips his coffee with an exaggerated, aggravating noise. "You must work for one of those private schools, if they're flying you business. Or is it family money?"

Why don't you take a nice, loud slurp of boiling hot *shut the fuck up and mind your own business*? "It's work."

He nods his approval. "You must be doing all right. Me," he laughs, "I just needed to get away. Work is such a great excuse." He accepts the offer of a second coffee from the fight attendant. "You wouldn't believe it," he says, "but this is peaceful compared to home." The plane shudders and lurches, as if to underline just how shitty home must be.

"She keeps pets. *In the kitchen*."

He pauses for effect. Perhaps he's hoping she's imagining a litter box under the kitchen table, a dog lifting its leg on the fridge, a ferret roaming the bench tops.

"Goldfish."

She wants so badly to put her headphones on and listen to a book.

"A tank with two fish in it. And she *talks* to them. And their names are Huckleberry and Tim." He pauses for a beat, anticipating confusion that she doesn't feel. "Because 'Finn.' Get it?"

Thank you for explaining that.

"But that's not—"

The plane slams into a downdraft and loses three hundred metres in the blink of an eye. Breakfast dishes shout in protest, coffee hot enough to annoy splashes across his wrist, all the warning lights go on and the captain murmurs an announcement reminding them to stay seated and with their seatbelts on.

He mops at the coffee, unperturbed. "So the fish change. They change every two or three months. Because she's bad at looking after them. Probably shouldn't keep them right next to the microwave. I reckon she nukes them. One week Tim's orange and white, and the next thing, he's got black dots. Or a double tail. Or googly eyes. It doesn't seem to matter that she keeps killing them off, she just has to have them there. To talk to."

It's probably the best conversation his wife has, the only time she's ever listened to. She thinks of home. It isn't breakfast time there, she's already lost track of the hours, but she thinks of their morning routine. Of Max, warm from the shower and the ironically named Mittens, who does not have white paws, appearing like a little shadow in the kitchen. He will get his breakfast before the coffee even goes on. She thinks of that day at the animal shelter, Max cupping the tiny black bundle in his hand.

The sky is black now. No stars, just walls of cloud and a steady battering of hail. The flight attendants have packed everything away, including themselves. The plane shudders and lurches, tossed like a toy in the fist of the wind.

Pitch looks hard and solid at room temperature but if

struck by a hammer it's easily shattered.

"Looks like we're not going to be fed again any time soon." He spreads his blanket back across his lap and for a thrilling moment she thinks he's going to sleep. She reaches down towards her bag and he takes her hand. "We can think of something to do, though. Right?" He smiles at her, conspiratorially, intimately, and presses her hand into the soft bulge of his crotch.

Her reaction is unplanned, reflexive; snatching her hand away, slapping his face. But on the upswing, the grainy flesh of his jowl catches on the proud little solitaire of the engagement ring; presented to Melissa on a warm autumn evening. And as her palm connects with his face, her nail hooks the loose, grey skin at the corner of his eye, and now he's opened up in two directions.

His expression of open-mouthed, googly-eyed shock makes her think of a goldfish. A dead one. Her hands are shaking. His hands have blood on them. He gets up, despite the turbulence, despite the warnings, and staggers towards the toilet.

She imagines him angry, trying to re-open a freezer door on a hot day. She imagines him ignoring stop signs and red lights. She imagines him stepping into the sky outside and defying gravity for a moment, just like a cartoon character.

In a time-lapse movie, the pitch drop forms at the bottom of the funnel, a hard, cold globe that expands like a shiny turd. The neck of the drop draws and lengthens. Nobody has witnessed the fall. With the blow of a hammer, the drop would be shattered.

She imagines him in the bathroom, wiping away the blood and can only hope his dignity will prevent him from acknowledging that a woman could have done such harm.

She imagines him:

Abusive.

Pompous.

Going down!

"Pitch Drop"

AMANDA LE BAS DE PLUMETOT is an entertainment service provider living in Melbourne, Australia—although she's quick to point out the job's not so sexy as it sounds, and that really she's just a granny who sells popcorn at a cinema. She's had her short stories and poems published previously, including in *34 Stories*, the 2020 Literary Taxidermy Writing Competition anthology inspired by Aldous Huxley's *Brave New World*.

She says: "I'm very grateful to literary taxidermy for inspiring and challenging me to write again. For this story, it seemed to make sense to bring it into 2022 by turning Poe's character into an airline passenger, but it was the closing line that reminded me of the Pitch Drop experiment. I know, two things that really don't go together, but sometimes, an idea gets stuck there and just won't leave. The theme came from the nightmare of women's rights still being violated in so many countries."

Valparaiso

(Patricio Herrera, born in Chile 1849—died in Wales 1929.
Carolina Masafierro—details unknown.)

Of my country and of my family I have little to say.
One almost forgotten, the other far away.
But, Carolina, I remember Valparaiso,
How we used to stand, hand in hand,
On that tar and fish gut harbour,
The wide horizon and the sea.

I sailed at tide turn, with a promise, that on my return,
I would wear the white gloves of a Captain.
"Te amo"—I love you.
You said you would wait for me.
Weeks passed, months, a year.

I grew lonely.

I did not plan to make this place my home.
Landlocked, dry docked, in this coal town,
pocked and sunstarved vale.
In the belly of these black-seamed hills,
In Wales.

Your eyes were brown, hers were blue,
Yet something in her look reminded me of you.
Te amo—"I love you,"
The same words, a different tongue.
So long ago. I was foolish,
We were young.

I am, at heart, an honourable man.
I did the honourable thing.
Two witnesses, a borrowed suit,
A ring, and when the baby came
I forsook the ocean for a coal miner's life.

We have three more children now,
I speak to them in Spanish. I love my wife
But still I dream about you, Carolina.
I see you there on Valparaiso harbour,
The wide horizon and the sea.
Do you ever think of me?

And in the quiet of the night,
Can you hear the sound?
From the confines of this iron cage,
The distant echo of my heartbeat,
In the darkness, going down!

"Valparaiso"

TRUDI PETERSEN is a nurse and shop owner living in Wales in the United Kingdom. She grew up in Laugharne—the home of the Welsh writer Dylan Thomas—so poetry, she tells us, has always been close to her heart. She has been previously published in *Shot Glass Review*, *Red Poets*, and the *Welsh Poetry Competition* anthology. Her poem, "Valparaiso," is a poignant story of love, both lost and found. It captures in a mere thirty-nine lines a story that is romantic, wistful, heartbreaking, and ineluctably human. Poe's first and last lines frame the narrative perfectly, and the piece is an excellent example of the transformative power of literary taxidermy. It was a joy to read and a pleasure to award.

She says: "I am slightly obsessed with family history, and this was the spark for my poem. It's based on the true story of my great, great, grandfather who came from an aspirational Chilean family. He was meant to marry Carolina whom he had known since childhood. Instead, he fell in love with a local Welsh girl—my great, great, grandmother. He became a coal miner, raising a family of six in a tiny two-roomed terraced cottage. He never went 'home.' I have a letter that Carolina wrote to him. The line about the white gloves comes from a comment she made. He never forgot her. Their story passed down the generations to me."

C.S. Griffel

Epsilon-581

Of my country and of my family, I have little to say. All memory of them was wiped from my mind. Except, it hadn't worked; at least, not entirely. I dreamed of them. There were trees in my dreams dotting the landscape of green hills, often dense enough to obscure the sky until they broke away into a field of gentle, low hills carpeted in green. It must have been my home, but I had not been there in a long time.

A mother with dirty blond hair and pale blue eyes stroked my face when I slept. I knew she was my mother by the intensity of love in her eyes as she gazed at me. She spoke to me, but her voice came to me muffled. Her presence shimmered and vanished into mist before I could ever make out the words. I would wake, beating my pillow, calling out, "What did you say, Mother?"

Other nights, I ran across grass-covered hills, frequently glancing over my shoulder. Someone was chasing me, but I was unafraid. I caught only glimpses of a dark-haired man whose laughter filled the air. As I laughed in return, he called to me but the word was muffled. Was it "Sarah"? I couldn't be sure. Is my name Sarah? Farah? Clara?

Waking from one such dream, I stirred in my bed. I was in a small room painted white. My sheets, blankets, and pillows were so perfectly white that it was difficult to differentiate one from another. Still, the pillows could not quite meet the stark whiteness of the walls.

A nurse dressed in a white, knee-length tunic entered my room without knocking. No such privacy was afforded any of us. Most of the other subjects didn't have enough recall to be irritated by the lack of nicety. My eyes narrowed as she entered, but I had long ceased complaining. I learned quickly not to reveal how much I remembered.

The nurse moved across the room in bright white shoes, white hose, with her hair tucked under a white headcover, leaving only her face and hands exposed.

"Epsilon-581, it's time to get up," she instructed me.

"Yes, Nurse Jones." I clambered out of bed. Our beds were one of the greatest luxuries afforded us; they were large and soft, the kind of bed made for encouraging deep and dreamless sleep.

While Nurse Jones scanned the machinery monitoring my health, I pulled a white cotton shift over my head. As the fabric fell softly over my body, I unconsciously ran my fingers over the small lump in my left forearm. This is where the chip had been placed that linked to the monitors.

"How did you sleep?" she asked.

"Fine." We both knew it was a lie. She could see from the readings my sleep had been restless.

"Hmm," she replied, "perhaps we need to recommend a sleep aid."

I rolled my eyes. I didn't want a sleep aid, but it was useless to argue.

"It's a big day today," she chirped.

"A big day. Sure," I responded.

"Yes. Madame President will be arriving for her infusion today." Nurse Jones spoke as though it were exciting news. She didn't have to endure the infusion process as I did. "It is a great honor to be chosen, Epsilon-581. Make sure to show gratitude when you meet her." I had nothing to say so I simply gave a single nod of my head. To her, it was a big day, an honor, but to me, it was the beginning of my end.

Heading to the cafeteria, Nurse Jones instructed, "You must eat well this morning. You'll need your strength and

Madame President needs the nutrition."

The cafeteria was filled with girls all dressed the same as me. I can't say how old the youngest were, I didn't know how old I was. My few memories were sketchy, and I didn't have a way to count time. It was not something allowed to us.

Everything in the facility was meant to keep the subjects passive. Everything was as white as they could manage, because color contains memory. The food was unseasoned because taste contains memory. We weren't allowed outside because light and sound contain memory. Memory contains longing. Longing contains discontent. Discontent breeds rebellion.

The food we ate was the only thing that had any color anywhere, aside from our skin. Rather than oatmeal, I was served a rare steak with eggs and crispy potatoes and a glass of orange juice. Despite the lack of seasoning, it was, admittedly a treat.

My only friend, Zeta-176, sat next to me with her bowl of mush.

"Are you scared?" she asked.

I shrugged. "I don't want it to be my turn if that's what you're asking me. But I am tired of this place. Perhaps it will be a relief."

"I'll miss you."

Zeta-176 wiped at her damp eyes. The words "it's going to be okay" stuck in my throat. That was a lie. It wasn't going to be okay. Her turn would come, the same as mine had. Then her blood would be slowly drained from her body over the course of several days, recycled and processed to become the elixir infused into Madame President. It was an honor, we were told, to keep Madame President alive. If not for our sacrifice and that of the many who came before, Madame President would die, and then where would the nation be? The people needed Madame President. The people loved Madame President. If they didn't, why had they just voted for her 47th term in office?

Nurse Jones approached the table. "It's time," she said. I wasn't the only girl whose number had come up. We were chosen in groups of ten. The girls in the room fell silent, eyes turned to those of us standing to be escorted to the great hall. It was not customary to say goodbye. Only Zeta-176 moved. She hugged me, brushed away her tears, and smiled.

I tried to smile in return, but I know it must have looked horribly awkward. My smile didn't come from anywhere inside me, except the place where I wanted Zeta-176 to stop crying.

We didn't go straight to the procedure room. First came the pomp and circumstance. We made our way to the great hall to await Madame President's arrival. I was the first to arrive so I could take my place in the front row from where I would be escorted to the dais after Madame President's arrival. There, I would bow low before her and offer myself up for the good of the nation.

The rest of the hall filled with nurses and girls. The large room hummed with whispered conversations, shuffling feet and gently whooshing fabric as everyone came in and found seats. The room grew still as Nurse Riley, the head nurse, made her way to the crystalline podium at the center of the dais. Rows of chairs for Madame President's entourage flanked it. Nurse Riley cleared her throat before speaking.

"In the grand tradition of this institution, established long ago with Madame President Dabria's first infusion, we welcome you again today to witness the brave young women who will bring forward their very lifeblood as a tribute to our glorious nation. As we know, President Dabria has sacrificed her own death to live for the sake of the nation. The nation is Dabria and Dabria is the nation."

In unison, the entire room responded, "The nation is Dabria and Dabria is the nation."

As Nurse Riley closed her speech, the Presidential Guard marched onto the dais. Their entrance was uniform. Someone began chanting "Dabria." The room joined in until the cry "Dabria" thundered through the space. To me, they sounded like automatons, capable of responding to stimuli, yet lifeless. I suppose I should have been panicking; after all, I didn't want to die, only, I didn't think there was any point in it.

President Dabria, dressed in the same stark white as her guard, gracefully made her way onto the dais. Her hair was also a beautiful snowy white, framing a face that should have long ago shriveled away to a white skull, but instead retained a youth stolen from generations of young women like me. She raised a hand to quiet the crowd, "Bring the tributes forward."

Nurse Jones took me by the arm, leading me to the line of nine other girls. We joined hands and made our way forward. We formed a semicircle around the front of the dais, our faces towards President Dabria. As if one person, we all knelt, raising our hands, still clinging to one another as if in an ancient worship ritual.

Nurse Riley, her countenance grave, signaled to us to rise. We rose as one, continuing to cling to one another's hands, and marched from the stage.

The infusion process was not so much painful as it was exhausting. The first round of blood cleansing complete, we were sent back to our rooms. Not all of us would make it past the second cleansing. None of us would make it past the third.

Drained, I drifted quickly to sleep. My mother came to me. The dark-haired man was with her and I knew that he was my father. As I lay in bed, she sat on its edge and stroked my face. "Zara"—her voice was not muffled, but clear and lovely—"wake up, Zara, it's time to go." She smiled down at me, as did my father. He then stood and began packing a small bag before hiking it over his shoulders and onto his back. I noticed that their glances at one another were furtive. Something was wrong, but they were not letting me in on the secret. The two of them moved quickly; my mother handed me clothes. "You must dress warmly, darling. We're going on a long, lovely hike. *Quickly now.*"

There was noise from outside. My father froze and the color drained from his face. He and my mother exchanged one long look, before he said, "Stay here," and left the room. I heard shouting before there was silence.

"Zara, get in the closet, hide, and don't make a sound. No matter what happens. Not one sound." She shoved me in as the door of my room burst open. I could see through small slats in the door. Two men, armed with small swords entered. My mother, standing to her full height, faced them.

"Where is the child?" they demanded.

"Gone. I sent her through the window." One of the men raised his sword above my mother's head. I was terrified. I gasped. The man's eyes shot to the closet door. He seemed to be looking straight into my eyes. My mother never even glanced towards me. She continued to stare straight at the man. She gave no sign of my location, but it was too late. The man slashed the sword, striking her. My mother's body slumped and fell to the ground.

My screaming woke me from sleep. My face was wet with tears. My mother. My father. Soon, I would join them. I would maintain my dignity, as I had maintained my fragments of memory. I would go to my death gladly, knowing they hadn't been able to erase me from my own mind. I thought of my mother as I had last seen her—going down.

"Epsilon-581"

C.S. GRIFFEL is an English professor living in Texas in the United States. But being a college professor is her second career. She spent twenty years homeschooling her children which she says is the best and most important thing she's ever done. She loves live theatre and has started two theatre companies, directing several shows. She has been previously published in *The Talon Review* and *After Dinner Conversation*.

She says: "When I read the Poe prompt, the next words popped into my head instantly. I knew then that the story had a sci-fi vibe. I wrote the first version quickly, in less than an hour. I shared the first version of the story with an online critique group. After some excellent feedback about the grandiose ending, I edited the story and changed the ending. I made a few final edits, crossed my fingers, and submitted."

Gail Ingram

Aotearoa, the Land
of the Milk White Proud

Of my country and of my family
I have little to say
Of the little and the quiet life
I have led
I have followed
My family and my country
Who have led us
To believe how peaceful we are
How green! How beautiful!
My mother cries
All those cows!
How green with envy you outsiders look!
For we have milk
We have so much milk to sell you
For a good price!
My brother cries
We have water
So much water to give away
In plastic bottles
To big countries with no
Morals! It is free!
My country cries

It flows from the melting ice
It flows freely down
To the cows! The beautiful cows!
It flows into our deep aquifers
Where the little drips
Of nitrogen and plastic
Also flow. To keep the grass
Growing!
My brother says
How green! It's okay
My country says
The plastic weedmat the council lays
It's okay
The nitrogen fertilizer the farmer sprays
It will go down
Down
Down our throats
Our throats are filling
With gratitude for milk
And nitrogen!
And plastic!
Good for your bones!
My father says
We are trying to speak
How green we are
How peaceful our neighbours
Our little island neighbours in the Pacific
Our little island neighbours who can't afford our milk

Our throats are too swollen to say
Our little neighbours are sinking
Under the weight of my country's water
They are surrounded
With little drips
We won't drown!
We're not little drips!
Of my family and of my country I can say

How beautiful! How green!
We're not going down!

"Aotearoa, the Land of the Milk White Proud"

GAIL INGRAM is a poet, editor, and teacher living in Christchurch, New Zealand. She tells us that her secret power is jiggling. While jiggling she can be mum, lover, have five jobs, and sneak time for those pleasurable things, such as words and admiring the wee flowers on weeds. She has been previously published in multiple anthologies, including *Poetry New Zealand*, *Landfall*, *takahē*, *Love in the Time of Covid*, and *Catalyst*, among others.

She says: "This was one of those poems that my pen wrote all by itself. Once my trusty green biro picked up on the tone of Poe's lines, off it went. I grew up in the heart of Te Waipounamu, the South Island high country, where the hills used to sway with golden tussock. In my lifetime, the tussock herb fields have been degraded to almost a dust bowl because of New Zealand's insatiable need to produce wool, then milk, at all costs."

Lina

"Of my country and of my family I have little to say. And I don't like people who are too interested in either," Sanchez said.

His voice sounded far away and the jackhammer in my head was loud enough to wake half the state. I had a vague recollection of a blunt object hitting me in the back of the head. The jackhammer only got worse when I opened my eyes. Colors bled into each other, and the whole room looked like Van Gogh's *Starry Night.*

Alejandro Sanchez, the eloquent gentleman who wasn't happy with my inquiries into his past, stood a few feet away from me on the other side of a table. To his left was a goliath of a man, wearing a suit and carrying a gun. From the look in his eyes, I could tell that words over one syllable would overheat his brain.

The room we were in was behind the bar where I had been inquiring about Sanchez. It was a dingy room, consisting of stacked boxes, mousetraps, an old sink, and cheap lighting.

I tried to stand up, and I discovered my hands were tied behind me to a chair. On the table were the contents of my pockets: my wallet, my .45, and a photograph. At present, Sanchez was spinning my .45 on the table. I was hoping he'd shoot himself by accident, then I could escape while his trained monkey tried to think for himself.

"Guns are dangerous, Mr. Locke," Sanchez said as he reached for my wallet.

"Only to Neanderthals. And I have a license for that," I said between jackhammer impacts.

"And for being a private detective, it seems," Sanchez replied, leaving the gun and flicking through my wallet

I shrugged as best I could.

"But most interesting," he continued, "is *this*."

He held up the photograph—and old one of a twenty-something man with an impressive mustache. The young man bore a striking resemblance to Sanchez, though Sanchez was at least in his fifties and had no mustache.

"So, what's a gringo private detective doing with an old picture of me? And why is this private detective asking for information about me?"

I really could have gone for a double scotch right about then. "I freelance as a census taker," I said.

The goliath punched me in the face, breaking my nose, and it didn't do my headache a whole lot of good.

"I'm sorry," I said. "I meant, *go fuck yourself.*"

The second punch realigned my nose a bit.

"Client privilege," I said through my bleeding nose. "I can't go around telling everyone my client's names. Bad for business."

In this case, my client was a lovely twenty-five-year-old woman named Lina. But they didn't need to know that yet. Sanchez sat across from me and smirked.

"Mr. Locke," he said. "Years ago, in Columbia, we didn't waste time with these sorts of niceties. Have you ever seen someone dissolved in acid while they're alive?"

I stared back at him, hoping he couldn't see the combination of hatred and fear that was percolating in my throbbing head.

"Sometimes," he continued, "we'd capture people and make them fight to the death with baseball bats. Anyone who didn't fight, we shot."

"Surprised you don't have a lot more major league

baseball players," I said. "You're saying a lot for having little to say about your country."

Sanchez smiled, or at least he mimicked the gesture as best as he could to somehow appear human. "This is America," he said. "And it's not the early '90s anymore. It's a lot more of a hassle to disappear people. Not impossible. Just a hassle. Or maybe I'm just getting old. What do you think, Carlos?"

The goliath/Carlos said nothing.

"Carlos is a good man," Sanchez continued. "He doesn't give his opinion even when asked for it. Anyway, Mr. Locke, let's try again. Why were you looking for me?"

I wanted nothing more than to put a .45 round right through his smug face. I'd make sure to shout out a multisyllabic word beforehand to confuse Carlos. As much as I wanted to protect Lina, I figured it was best to give Sanchez something to chew on. I couldn't protect Lina if I got myself dead.

"A girl hired me to look for you," I said.

"Why?"

"Because she thinks you're her father."

I saw Sanchez's demeanor waver. It wasn't much. Just the slightest twitch under his left eye. Carlos remained stoic. Sanchez looked down at the table, then back at me. "Explain yourself."

For a brief moment, I considered pointing out that we could have avoided all of this excitement (particularly my concussion) had he asked this before having Carlos club me into oblivion. My head still hurt, so I opted to give Sanchez the short version.

"She's the one who gave me the picture," I said. "She told me she thought her father was dead. That her mother took her away years ago. All she had was the picture, and the name on the back of it. She saw you about a week ago, but she wasn't sure. So she figured hiring a detective would help her be more sure. Hopefully you'll be nicer to her than you were to me."

Sanchez's demeanor wavered again, and, for the first time, he looked like an old man. The hardened exterior melted away, if only for a moment, and I'm pretty sure I saw what remained of his humanity. Even Carlos had raised an eyebrow. He had probably never seen his boss express any sort of vulnerability.

Sanchez looked at Carlos, then back to me. "Impossible. My daughter was taken from me a long time ago by my *puta* of a wife. Why would I believe it's really her?"

"How the hell should I know?" I said. "I'm a private detective, not a social worker. Her money was good. That's all that mattered."

Sanchez's eyes narrowed, and he bunched his hands into fists. I braced myself for the inevitable punch. Instead, he looked at Carlos and gave a slight nod. Carlos came over and cut the ropes on my wrists. I reached for my wallet and my gun as casually as I could. Carlos's hand came down on mine as I gripped the .45.

"Too much paperwork if I shoot you," I said.

Carlos looked at Sanchez, who nodded again. Carlos released my hand, and I put my .45 back into my shoulder holster. Sanchez threw a towel at me. "Clean yourself up." he said.

I went to the sink, soaked the towel, then did my best to get the blood off. My nose was definitely broken, but the cold water eased my headache for a few moments.

"Are there any markings on this girl?" Sanchez asked.

My head was still swimming, but I managed to tread water. "Yeah." I said. "A scar under her left eye. Looks like she got it as a child."

"Is her name Lina?"

"Yes."

"*Es ella*...please, take me to her. You understand, all of this. It's—"

"Business. Yeah. Never gets old. She's staying at a hotel near here. You gonna take the gorilla with you?"

"I didn't live this long by being foolish."

"Fair enough."

When we got to the hotel, I called Lina from the lobby to see if she was there, which she was. I told her I'd found him, giving all the relevant details, and I heard such jubilation in her voice that I couldn't help but think how disappointed she'd be when she saw what a thug her father was. I told her we'd be right up. Sanchez, Carlos, and I all crammed into the elevator and rode up to the fourteenth floor.

I knocked on her door, and she opened it. She was wearing a knee-length skirt, a blouse, and open-toed heels, looking absolutely stunning. Of course, she was the sort of girl who would look stunning wearing a trash bag. Carlos barged past her and surveyed the room and the bathroom. He turned to Sanchez and nodded. Sanchez hesitated, then took a step into the room. I followed and shut the door behind me.

Lina had walked back to the bureau, and Sanchez followed. He stood opposite her and put his hands on her shoulders. Gently, he ran his finger across the scar under her eye. "You cut yourself with your fingernail by accident when you were only two. I could never believe it would leave a scar," he said.

Tears brewed in Lina's eyes and ran down her face. "It's really you," she said.

In the next few seconds, two things happened. First, a bullet exited Sanchez's back. Then, a second bullet struck Carlos in the right eye, spraying his limited mental abilities all over the wall.

Sanchez collapsed, still alive, and Lina stood over him, grasping a Colt 9mm Double Eagle. I pulled my .45 and pointed it at Lina, who looked back at me with tears still flowing down her face. Sanchez wheezed as the life bled out of him.

"He's not my father," Lina said to me, but she looked at Sanchez. "My real name isn't Lina. It's not so hard to change your name. He killed my family in Columbia. I was ten. I had been playing in the tall grass, when this *joto sicario* and his thugs came to our house, so they missed me. My father wouldn't join their cartel. He was a good man. I watched this *joto* cut my little brother Enrique's arms and legs off with an ax. He was six. And he made my parents watch."

Sanchez coughed, and blood sprayed out of his mouth, spattering on Lina's legs. She put her heeled foot onto the bullet wound. Sanchez groaned in pain.

"But...," he whimpered, "the scar—"

"I did it myself. With a razor. And I found out where your real daughter was."

"What did you do to her?"

"I did to her what you did to my brother," she said. "And I brought some souvenirs."

Lina reached into the bureau and tossed some white objects onto his chest. Teeth.

Sanchez tried to get up, but Lina kicked him. Now it was Sanchez's turn to cry. I heard him mumble, "*Mi hija...mi hija....*" right before Lina shot him in the head.

She closed her eyes for a moment, then looked at me and said, "There is twenty-one thousand dollars in my purse over there for you. I'm sorry I lied to you. I had to."

With my .45 still trained on her, I said, "Maybe this piece of shit deserved it, but his daughter didn't."

Through the tears, Lina laughed. "I bought those teeth at a junk shop. They're plaster. His daughter is safe with her mother, completely oblivious to all of this. I needed him to feel a little of the pain I felt. And he has. And now it's over."

She placed the Colt on the bureau, then went to the bed and lay down. I walked over to her purse and opened it. There was a huge wad of cash in there. I pulled it out. Under the rubber band was an address for a Lina Rojos. I took a thousand out of the wad for myself. Twenty-one thousand was far too much.

I grabbed the room phone and called the police. I told them all the important stuff. Then I hung up and lay on the bed next to Lina. She moved over to me and rested her head on my shoulder.

"Thank you," she said.

My headache had caught up with me again. I don't know when I fell asleep. I dreamed of Sanchez in a burning elevator. Going down.

"Lina"

SAM BSHERO is a high school English teacher living in Pennsylvania in the United States. He tells us that he enjoys reading works of both fiction and nonfiction, listens to heavy metal music (including bands whose lead singer "sounds like a malfunctioning garbage disposal"), and knows way too much about movies. "Lina" is his first published story.

He says: "At first, my thinking involved trying to figure out what sort of person nowadays would say that opening line. Then followed notes, frustration, and more notes. To force myself into a genre (so I could avoid more indecisiveness), I settled on detective fiction since I like Raymond Chandler. That said, this is the first mystery I've ever written."

Appendix 1

Honorable Mentions

We received nearly a thousand entries in this year's Literary Taxidermy Writing Competition, and many impressed both early readers and final judges. In the end many good stories and poems were turned away. The following entries all made it to the last round of selection. Keep an eye out for these writers. We're confident you'll see their work in the future.

Short Stories

Julia Brieger, "The Flooding"
Kim Dicso, "Son of a Beth"
Rhonda Valentine Dixon, "Going Down"
Evan Gillespie, "Disgruntled Short Story"
Ruth Goldberg, "Bloodlines"
Trudy Graham, "Choices"
Jacqui Greaves, "You Are Already Dead"
Melissa Gunn, "Seeds of Hope"
Emily Hanlon, "Eclipsed"
Margo Karolyi, "Into the Woods"
Simon King, "Heed the Silent"
Michael Kuty, "Beach Blanket Bloodshed"
Charlin McIsaac, "Uncle Liam's Iron Foot"
Melanie McKerchar, "Geophagy"
Sue Scarlett Montgomery, "End the Patriarchy"
Adrian F. Roscher, "At Bergdorf's"

Maria Rybakova, "Shameshame"
Andrea L. Staum, "The Wretched Bond"
Lisa VanGalen, "Endings, Beginnings,
                                    and Something In Between"
Kyle Woods, "10,000 Years of Darkness"

Poetry

Helen Anderson, "Findlings"
Goh Yong Ming Calvin, "Foreword"
Steven Case, "Neptune's Chains"
Danielle Davey, "*Le Ballet de la Nuit*"
Sean Fallon, "First Words"
Hawk and Young, "Schrödinger's Bomb Shelter"
Susan Jane Hay, "Elevated Conversation"
Catherine Lee, "Dreams of Master's Sons
                                    or Whirling Sun?"
Sean McConville, "The Ballad of John Jacob Finnegan"
Paul Joseph Rodriguez, "The Collector"

This Year's Judges

Given our desire for submissions to span genres, we assembled a group of professional writers and editors from all walks of the literary life. The judges for this year's competition included poets, novelists, a playwright, mystery writers, a memoirist, a humorist, and the winning author from one of our previous competitions. They all had a challenging task, separating not only wheat from chaff, but wheat from wheat, and we are grateful for their enthusiastic and perspicacious participation.

Catherine Barnett is the author of three collections of poems: *Human Hours* (2018), *The Game of Boxes* (2012), and *Into Perfect Spheres Such Holes Are Pierced* (2004). Her honors include a Whiting Award, a Guggenheim Fellowship, and the James Laughlin Award from the Academy of American Poets. She has published widely in journals and magazines, including *The American Poetry Review*, *Barrow Street*, *The Iowa Review*, *The Kenyon Review*, and *The Washington Post*. Barnett teaches in the graduate and undergraduate programs at New York University, is a distinguished lecturer at Hunter College, and works as an independent editor. She has degrees from Princeton University, where she has taught in the Lewis Center for the Arts, and from the MFA Program for Writers at Warren Wilson College.

Cuifen Chen is a writer from Singapore. Her short fiction has been published in print anthologies and online, while her poetry has appeared in the *Southeast Asian Review of English* and her creative nonfiction in *Fourth Genre*. Cuifen was the winner of the Troubadour International Poetry Prize in 2018 and the Literary Taxidermy Short Story Competition in 2019. Most recently, she received an Honourable Mention (English Short Story Category) in the Golden Point Award, Singapore's premier creative writing competition. Cuifen holds a MA with Distinction in Creative Writing from LASALLE College of the Arts. She likes role-playing games, visual novels, liminal spaces, and most of all fantastic things.

Elisa Donovan is an American actress, writer, and mother. She played the role of Amber in the 1995 teen comedy film *Clueless* and in the TV series of the same name. Donovan went on to play the role of Morgan Cavanaugh in the sitcom *Sabrina the Teenage Witch*. She has had pieces published in the "Chicken Soup for The Soul" series, and has spoken about recovery on many television shows including 20/20, Entertainment Tonight, and Headline News. Donovan's first book, *Wake Me When You Leave*, is a personal memoir about losing her job, a relationship, and her father to cancer. By sharing the lessons and challenges of loss, Donovan inspires those who are learning to let go. The film version of *Wake Me When You Leave*, currently in development, will mark Elisa's screenwriting and directorial debuts.

Danny Gardner is an American writer, actor, stand-up comic, and director. He is a Pushcart Prize nominee for his creative non-fiction piece "Forever. In an Instant.," published by *Literary Orphans Journal*. His first short fiction piece, "Labor Day," appeared in *Beat to a Pulp*, and his flash fiction has been featured in *Out of the Gutter* and on *Noir on the Air*. He is the author of the Black American mystery series *The Tales of Elliot Caprice*—including the novels *A Negro and an Ofay* and *Ace Boon Coon*—which features disgraced Chicago Police Officer Elliot Caprice. He is a frequent reader at Noir at the Bar events nationwide, blogs regularly at 7 Criminal Minds, and is a proud member of the Mystery Writers of America and the International Thriller Writers. Danny lives in Los Angeles by way of Chicago.

Rick Moody is an American novelist and short story writer. His first novel, *Garden State*, was the winner of the 1991 Editor's Choice Award from the Pushcart Press and was published in 1992. *The Ice Storm* was published in 1994 (and then turned into a film of the same name, directed by Ang Lee). His short fiction and journalism have been anthologized in *Best American Stories 2001*, *Best American Essays 2004*, *Best American Essays 2008*, and *Year's Best Science Fiction #9*, among others. His radio pieces have appeared on The Next Big Thing, Re:Sound, Weekend America, Morning Edition, and at the Third Coast International Audio Festival. In May 2018 he received an Award in Literature from the American Academy of Arts and Letters. In 2019 he became an *Officier de L'Ordre des Arts et des Lettres*, as awarded by the Republic of France.

Brian Parks is an American playwright and editor. He lives in New York City and served as the Arts & Culture editor at *The Village Voice*. His plays have been produced in the U.S. as well as in the UK, Ireland, Australia, New Zealand, Germany, Austria, and Switzerland. His play *Americana Absurdum* helped launch the New York International Fringe Festival, where it also won the Best Writing Award. *Americana Absurdum* went on to win a Fringe First award at the 2000 Edinburgh Festival Fringe and became one of the first plays staged at London's Menier Chocolate Factory theater. His play *Enterprise* won a Fringe First Award at the 2017 Edinburgh Festival Fringe. A Detroit-area native, he's been a longtime resident of Brooklyn.

Michael Pronko is a mystery writer, essayist, and teacher, born in Kansas City, but living and writing in Tokyo for the past twenty years. He has published three award-winning collections of essays: *Beauty and Chaos: Essays on Tokyo*; *Motions and Moments: More Essays on Tokyo*; and *Tokyo's Mystery Deepens*. His award-winning mystery series—including *The Last Train*, *The Moving Blade*, *Tokyo Traffic*, and *Tokyo Zangyo*—features Detective Hiroshi Shimizu who investigates white collar crime in Tokyo. He writes regularly for many publications, including *The Japan Times*, *Newsweek Japan*, *Jazznin*, *Jazz Colo[u]rs*, and *Artscape Japan*; and runs his own website, Jazz in Japan. He is a professor of American Literature at Meiji Gakuin University where he teaches seminars in contemporary novels and film adaptations.

Cameron Tuttle is the author of the bestselling series *The Bad Girl's Guides* and *The Paranoid's Pocket Guide*. Her books have been translated into 14 languages and inspired a Webby-nominated online community, an appearance on The Oprah Winfrey Show, a TV sitcom, a lawsuit, and countless fender benders. Tuttle also authored two angst-ridden, humorous YA novels, *Paisley Hanover Acts Out* and *Paisley Hanover Kisses and Tells*. She is currently writing a novel that's not the least bit funny. In addition to being a bestselling author, she's also a natural redhead, a California native, a content strategist, and an accidental entrepreneur.

You, Too, May Become a Literary Taxidermist!

All of us at Regulus Press wish to extend our thanks and appreciation to everyone who participated in the 2022 Literary Taxidermy Writing Competition. Your enthusiasm and commitment continue to exceed our expectations.

If you didn't participate this year and are coming to this collection of stories new to the idea of literary taxidermy, we hope you've enjoyed what you've found. And if you're a writer, we encourage you—the present reader—to become a future literary taxidermist.

This is our fifth year running the competition, and we're hoping to do it again, so we're looking for writers, both amateur and professional, to stitch together new and imaginative stories and poems. The competition is your chance to get your hands dirty and join the growing community of literary taxidermists.

For the latest on the competition (and to learn more about the possibilities of literary taxidermy), visit:

www.literarytaxidermy.com

We look forward to seeing what you stitch together!

About the Editor

Mark Malamud is a tail-end baby-boomer, writer, poet, inventor, puzzle-maker, designer, futurist, former software developer, and master dogsbody. His collection of short stories, *The Gymnasium*, established the idea of literary taxidermy. His most recent work, *The Timeless Machine*, transforms H.G. Wells' classic novella into a meditation on the limitations and contradictions of living with grief. He is principal and manager of busymonster, LLC, a consultancy company focused on advanced user interface and design. He holds over 700 patents, and in 2012 he was the 8th most-prolific inventor of patents in the US. His interests include kindness, turmoil, suspension of disbelief, and love.

The editor would like to offer his profound thanks to Sara Waits, Paul Van Zwalenburg, Donna Jean, and everyone at Regulus Press. This couldn't happen without you!

Literary Taxidermy from Regulus Press

The Art of Death

An anthology of literary taxidermy based on two works by New Zealand modernist Katherine Mansfield—the poem "The Black Monkey" and the short story "*Je ne parle pas français.*" Award-winning stories and poems from the 2021 Literary Taxidermy Writing Competition.

34 Stories

An anthology of literary taxidermy based on the first and last lines of *Brave New World* by Aldous Huxley. From a boy witch to a parental cyborg, from a woman trapped beneath a building to a lonely empress on a faraway planet—award-winning stories from the 2020 Literary Taxidermy Writing Competition.

Pleasure to Burn

An anthology of literary taxidermy based on the first and last lines of *Fahrenheit 451* by Ray Bradbury. From cheerful cannibals to transhuman plastivores—award-winning stories from the 2019 Literary Taxidermy Writing Competition.

The Gymnasium

Nineteen tales of melancholy and wonder by Mark Malamud, created by "re-stuffing" what goes in-between the opening and closing lines of classic works by Milan Kundera, Philip K. Dick, Thomas Wolfe, Ian Fleming, and others. The inspiration for the Literary Taxidermy Writing Competition.

www.regulus.press

Also by Mark Malamud

The Timeless Machine

The place is Richmond, a suburb of London. And something terrible—or wonderful—has happened. An English scientist, known only as the Time Traveler, has invented a machine . . . . Funny, clever, and heart-breaking, *The Timeless Machine* reshapes H. G. Wells' original novella into a story of madness and grief.

A Pocketful of Fish

A seaworthy celebration of dubious poetry, bringing together three previously-published collections of verse. Recipient of the National Poetry Award in 1974. Poetry by Choo 3T Fish. Edited by Mark Malamud and Tamara Croup.

On the Orient Express

By altering an event early in Christie's mystery—this time there is no murder—the remaining text must adjust to accommodate the absence of the crime. A transformation of the original novel into a narrative of redemption rather than revenge.

Labiovelora

Between the end of one day and the start of the next, there are twelve hidden hours, an interval perceived only by those born during midnight's midnight, also known as the *Labiovelora*. But those twelve hours are fragile, and it's up to one young woman—and the insatiable monster she carries inside her—to keep the *Labiovelora* safe.

www.regulus.press

Made in the USA
Las Vegas, NV
18 January 2023